"It happened so fast," she murmured.

"One moment you were the perfect assistant, and the next...the next, I didn't know what you were."

Donovan's eyes were veiled, oddly watchful, and that suddenly made Rebel nervous. "Don't look at me as though you're afraid of me, honey. It hurts."

"What do you want from me?" she asked in a whisper.

He hesitated, a flicker of indecision showing on his face. Then he sighed roughly. "The hell of it is," he muttered, "that I've waited a long time to answer that question, and now I know damn well you won't believe me."

Rebel was trying to understand what he meant when he pulled her forward abruptly and kissed her. His lips were warm, demanding, and achingly hungry. She couldn't help but respond...

Dear Reader:

Last month we were delighted to announce the arrival of TO HAVE AND TO HOLD, the thrilling new romance series that takes you into the world of married love. This month we're pleased to report that letters of praise and enthusiasm are pouring in daily. TO HAVE AND TO HOLD is clearly off to a great start!

TO HAVE AND TO HOLD is the first and only series that portrays the joys and heartaches of marriage. Its unique concept makes it significantly different from the other lines now available to you, and it offers stories that meet the high standards set by SECOND CHANCE AT LOVE. TO HAVE AND TO HOLD offers all the compelling romance, exciting sensuality, and heartwarming entertainment you expect.

We think you'll love TO HAVE AND TO HOLD—and that you'll become the kind of loyal reader who is making SECOND CHANCE AT LOVE an ever-increasing success. Read about love affairs that last a lifetime. Look for three TO HAVE AND TO HOLD romances each and every month, as well as six SECOND CHANCE AT LOVE romances each month. We hope you'll read and enjoy them all. And please keep writing! Your thoughts about our books are very important to us.

Warm wishes,

Ellen Edwards

Ellen Edwards
SECOND CHANCE AT LOVE
The Berkley Publishing Group
200 Madison Avenue
New York, N.Y. 10016

Second Chance at Love

KISSED BY MAGIC
KAY ROBBINS

A
SECOND CHANCE AT LOVE
BOOK

For
Alvin Robbins, my favorite uncle,
and
Brenda Robbins, my favorite fan.

"I daresay you haven't had much practice,"
said the Queen...
"Why, sometimes I've believed as many as six
impossible things before breakfast."

—Lewis Carroll

KISSED BY MAGIC

Chapter 1

REBEL READ THE final page of Knight's report and then lifted her head to glare across the desk at her executive assistant. "What is Lennox, anyway," she demanded irritably, "a dinosaur? I've seen more liberated views in my great-great-grandfather's diary!"

"He doesn't like dealing with women," Knight murmured. "Particularly female company presidents. He feels that a man should always have control. And he won't deal with a female executive. No exceptions."

The president of Sinclair Hotels flicked the neat papers in front of her with one short, unpolished nail. "Then I'm glad you'd heard those rumors about him," she said. "He certainly would have refused to sell that land to us if I'd approached him myself." She leaned back in her

comfortable chair and sighed. "Well, I shouldn't be surprised, I guess. I was bound to run into Lennox's type
sooner or later. I've just been lucky so far. I've been
president of this company for six months, and I hadn't
faced his kind of Neanderthal attitude yet. Dad warned
me to expect it, though."

"There aren't many of his type left," Knight pointed
out.

"No." Rebel studied her assistant, her customary abstraction lifting to reveal an unwontedly personal curiosity. "You're not his type, are you, Donovan?"

"I wouldn't work for you if I were." Donovan Knight
folded powerful arms across his massive chest and returned her gaze with the faintest hint of a smile.

"You were hired to work for my father when he was
president," she reminded him.

"But I stayed on when he retired. I could have left.
However, I happen to enjoy being your secretary."

"Executive assistant," she muttered, dismayed as always by the title he invariably gave himself.

"You're splitting hairs," he informed her calmly.
"Basically, I'm your secretary. I answer your mail, type
your letters, keep your appointments straight, et cetera."

He could have added, Rebel thought dryly, that he
did all those things—and more—with utter perfection.
In six months she had never seen the man make a single
mistake. Oddly irritated by the thought, she pushed it
aside.

Determinedly, she got the conversation back onto its
proper track. "About Lennox: How much do you think
he knows about Sinclair Hotels? Is he aware that I'm
president?"

Donovan shook his head slowly. "I don't think so."
A gleam of amusement lit his eyes briefly. "A good
secretary knows almost everything the boss knows, and
I spent some time talking to Lennox's secretary. She was

under the impression that Marc Sinclair still runs the company, since he's chairman of the board. And Lennox had been out of the country for months."

Rebel drummed her fingers lightly on the report on her desk, the shrewd business brain inherited from her father working keenly. "We must get that land," she murmured almost to herself. "We don't have a hotel in the Bahamas, and we need one there."

"And the project's your baby," Donovan offered.

Amused, she looked up to meet the shuttered violet eyes. In one neat sentence he'd eliminated the possibility of her running to her father for help. Not that she had any intention of doing so. She wondered why she didn't resent Donovan's pointing out the obvious.

"My baby," she agreed. "You and I have done the preliminary work, and everything's set—except the land. And, aside from the fact that I *want* that particular piece of land, the architect used it as a base for his plans. If we have to find land somewhere else, he'll probably have to revise considerably, if not start all over again."

"True. You were taking quite a gamble when you gave the architect the go-ahead."

"You're a lot of help," Rebel accused mildly. She lifted an eyebrow. "Let's hear some suggestions."

Donovan leaned back in his chair and crossed one leg over the other, drawing Rebel's gaze in spite of herself. She felt vaguely confused as she suddenly found herself watching the way his tailored business suit easily accommodated itself to his powerful muscles and graceful movements. What on earth was wrong with her? She'd never been distracted by his appearance before.

"You can't deal with Lennox directly," he said, cutting into her bewildered thoughts. "He'd refuse to see you, and he wouldn't do it politely. You can't make the deal through lawyers or subordinates, because he wouldn't stand for that, either. It'll have to be a face-to-face meeting—a leisurely one, from what I hear—with the head of the company. He won't accept less."

"Wonderful." Rebel drummed her fingers again, mentally pushing aside the crazy idea that had just occurred to her. "You've told me what I can't do; now tell me what I *can* do."

Her one-of-a-kind executive assistant shrugged with a faint smile. Donovan at a standstill? Impossible! Rebel wondered why that unnerved her.

The bizarre idea popped up again, and this time she considered it a little more carefully. Could they pull it off? A lot would depend on Donovan, she realized. She didn't doubt his trustworthiness one bit. His willingness, though . . . And another point would be her ability to relinquish the reins of the company technically and temporarily.

"Where's Lennox now?" she asked.

"At his vacation lodge in the Bighorn Mountains of Wyoming." Donovan responded promptly. "According to his secretary, he'll be there for at least two weeks—and I'd hate to tell you what I had to do to get that information out of her."

Rebel wanted to ask—badly—but she swallowed the sharp question. "Is he known for being a hospitable host?" she asked instead.

"Oddly enough, yes. Normally he fills the lodge to the rafters with guests when he's there, but not this time. He's due to leave for Europe in two weeks; this stay at the lodge is shorter than average, I gather. Aside from a domestic staff, Lennox has only his son for company. The son's about my age, I believe."

"Is business taboo at the lodge?"

"The opposite, if anything."

Rebel turned the nagging idea over in her mind one more time, looking for potential pitfalls and embarrassing possibilities. Her fingers drummed again; it was her only nervous mannerism. Absently, she watched Donovan's eyes drop to consider the movement for a moment and then lift, shuttered as always, back to her face. She felt a flicker of curiosity about what he was thinking, and then dismissed it as unimportant.

"How do you feel," she asked slowly, "about a little underhanded, unscrupulous scheming?"

Something unreadable gleamed for an instant in the depths of his eyes. "I've got an open mind," he drawled.

Rebel silently examined the idea one last time, looking for unpleasant gremlins lurking about in dark corners. Well, dammit, what choice did she have? She had to have that land.

"If I gave you temporary power of attorney for myself and the company, would you be willing to make a deal with Lennox as acting head of Sinclair Hotels?" Her voice was even, her eyes probing his expressionless face.

As usual, he appeared to grasp instantly what she had in mind. Rebel reflected that it was gratifying to have an assistant who never asked, "What do you mean by that?"

Donovan nodded slowly. "Of course—provided we can pull it off. As long as Lennox is out of touch and doesn't find any reason to check up on the company, it should work. But remember, this hotel is your baby. Even though I've been in on the planning, there are some questions only you could answer at this stage. And I hear Lennox is a big one for questions; he'll want to know exactly what's being planned for the land before he agrees to any terms for selling it."

Rebel thought for a moment, silently acknowledging the truth of his words, then nodded to herself. She had made a decision. "All right then. I'll go along as your secretary; if anything crops up, I'll be on the spot."

If Donovan was surprised at her suggestion, he didn't betray it by so much as the flicker of an eyelash. "It should work," he said simply. Then he added in a warning tone, "But if it doesn't—if Lennox finds out about our role-reversal—he'll be mad as hell."

"If he finds out, let him be mad." Rebel's lips twisted wryly. "Any twentieth-century man with his archaic notions deserves a jolt now and then; he'll learn that a woman can be as ruthless as a man."

Donovan merely nodded and rose to his feet. "I'll send off a wire to the lodge; we should hear something by this afternoon."

"Fine. If we get an invitation, call Buddy and have him warm up the jet. I don't want to waste any more time than necessary in getting that land." As an afterthought she added, "I assume there's somewhere we can land the jet in Wyoming?" She spoke with the natural distaste of someone who had lived her entire life in urban areas; she couldn't help considering Wyoming the back of beyond.

His lips twitching slightly, Donovan murmured, "There's an international airport in Casper. The lodge is northwest of the city; we'll have to rent a car."

"We'll probably have to rent a snowplow," she retorted. "Wyoming in December—and in the mountains, no less!" She rubbed the tension-knotted muscles at the base of her neck, pushing aside the heavy coil of silver-blond hair lying in a smooth chignon.

Disregarding her sarcasm, Donovan asked a logical question. "How do I introduce you to Lennox?"

A point—and a good one. It would hardly do to be introduced as Rebel Sinclair! She'd reverted to her maiden name after the divorce. Why not use her married name in this little charade? At least something useful could be retrieved from her fiasco of a marriage. "I'll use my married name: Anderson."

Donovan exhibited no curiosity, although presumably

he wouldn't know that she'd been married. "Good enough. Single or married?"

"Single." Her voice was definite. She'd borrow the name, but she'd be damned if she'd reclaim the title.

"Right." He started for the door. "I'll send off that wire." With one hand on the brass door handle, he turned to look back at her as though struck with a sudden thought. "By the way—don't bother to change your appearance; you look as prim and efficient as any good secretary."

Rebel looked at him sharply, suspiciously, sensing criticism, but he seemed perfectly grave. "Right," she responded evenly.

Donovan left her office, closing the door softly.

Rebel drummed her fingers on the report still in front of her and stared at the closed door, trying vainly to shake off a sudden uneasy feeling. Without conscious direction, her mind flew back to her first meeting with Donovan Knight, more than a year before.

Loaded down with a pile of reports and statistics, she had literally run into the mountain of a man in the hall outside what was then her father's office. Other than astonishment at his size and a fleeting impression of startling violet eyes, Rebel had paid little attention to him. She'd been preoccupied with business.

Had they spoken? Probably. Yes, she remembered now. Stilted, faintly embarrassed conventionalities.

"Oh! Excuse me! So sorry..."

"Don't mention it. No, don't bend over—you'll only drop something else. I'll get it. There. Can you manage?"

"Yes, of course. Uh...thank you."

"My pleasure." A graceful, oddly old-world bow.

Rebel frowned. For someone who'd been preoccupied with business, she certainly remembered that brief conversation clearly!

She stirred restlessly in her chair and tried to determine

why she was so uneasy. Because of this business trip with Donovan? No; although the circumstances were somewhat different, this certainly wouldn't be their first trip together. And how many business lunches and practically all-night work sessions at her apartment had they shared during the past six months?

They had worked together like a well-practiced team from the very beginning. Donovan had become her right hand, and Rebel had never questioned that or looked any deeper. In all truth, she admitted to herself, she had never really seen him as a man. She'd been under a great deal of pressure since she'd taken over her father's chair as president. He'd been traveling and had left her alone to find her footing. And after three years with the company full-time, and summers during college, she was qualified. She had since proven that she could run the company.

So she was beginning to relax now. And in relaxing, she had discovered that her "secretary" was a very attractive man. No—she was splitting hairs again. The truth was, she silently acknowledged, that the man was devastatingly handsome. He was every woman's fantasy walking around on two legs.

Rebel frowned irritably and tried to shake off the thought. She wasn't interested in men at the moment; she had a company to run. And Donovan had never shown any interest in her as a woman. He treated her with respect, supplied her with information and shrewd, sound advice, and never stepped over the line between employer and employee.

And if she had gotten the impression from time to time that there was a teasing glint in his eyes, she had instantly banished it as a misconception.

Long hours of working closely together had put them on a first-name basis rather quickly, but neither had probed the other's personal life. Rebel knew that he wasn't married, was thirty-six years old, and lived here in Dallas—

all items from his sketchy personnel file. She knew that her father had been enormously impressed with Donovan—so much so that he had hired the younger man as his assistant after only a fifteen-minute interview.

And that was everything she knew—factually—about Donovan Knight.

Intuitively and from observation, she could make a few guesses. If there was a woman in his life, he kept her well hidden, and the lady was either a paragon of understanding about his long hours or she was slavishly devoted. Occasionally, Rebel had detected a faint Southern drawl, and she mentally made a stab at Virginia or North Carolina for his birthplace.

He drank brandy and occasionally beer, ate his steaks rare, disliked Chinese food. He drove a car well—and fast—was never rattled by anything or anyone, and had somehow amassed a great deal of knowledge about the hotel business somewhere along the way.

Rebel pushed away the thoughts. She had a lot to do if she was going to fly off to Wyoming for an unspecified length of time. There was the board meeting tonight; her father would be coming home for that. She would have to clear up all minor business matters on deck at the moment and instruct her staff whom to contact if there was trouble while she and Donovan were gone. It would certainly ruin everything if someone called or wired Rebel Sinclair at the lodge!

There was no time for personal curiosity or inexplicable uneasiness—only business.

The wire from Lennox came late that afternoon, a jovial invitation for Mr. Knight and his "assistant," Miss Anderson, to visit the lodge for a week or so to discuss the property in question.

After Donovan had returned to his own office to continue gathering the material they would need, Rebel frowned down at the wire for a moment and then reached to pick up her phone. She'd have to call Bessie and have her pack a suitcase.

Her hand stopped just short of the receiver, her mind flying back to Donovan's words of this morning: *You look as prim and efficient as any good secretary.*

Still frowning, Rebel rose from behind the modern and masculine oak desk and crossed the large room to the full-length mirror beside the compact bar in the corner.

Prim and efficient? Halting before the mirror, Rebel took a careful, considering look at her appearance. She looked like a businesswoman, she thought defensively. To be sure, the tailored skirt and blazer were a bit severe, and the neutral color was not terribly flattering, but the outfit was both functional and comfortable. And while the white blouse might be plain, it *was* silk.

She lifted a hand to tuck back a strand of silver-blond hair, simultaneously noting both her blunt, unpolished nails and the almost total lack of color in her face. She seldom bothered with makeup.

Rebel felt suddenly shaken. When had this begun happening? She couldn't remember a time in her adult life when she hadn't played up her femininity, her attractiveness. When had she become this — this caricature of a businesswoman? Was this what her father had meant when he had given her an odd look six months before and warned her not to let the business take her over?

Rebel bit her lip for a moment, then nodded decisively and went back to her desk. She sat down and picked up the phone, placing a call to her apartment. Her housekeeper answered and gave Rebel no opportunity to say more than hello.

"Mister Donovan called about the trip," Bessie said cheerfully, a slight Spanish accent tinging her voice even after forty years in Texas. "He told me you'd be leaving in the morning and what to pack."

Hesitating slightly, Rebel dismissed the question of just what Donovan had said to pack. "Bessie . . . pack a few pretty things this time, please. I'm getting a little tired of suits."

"About time, too." Bessie sniffed. "You'll never catch another husband wearing those drab suits, Miss Rebel."

"I don't want another husband, Bessie," Rebel responded dryly. "I'm quite happy with the company."

"Well and good, Miss Rebel, but a company can't keep you warm at night," Bessie said flatly.

Rebel sighed and abandoned the familiar debate. "Never mind. Just pack the case. Oh, and keep out that dark blue dress I bought a while back; I'll wear that for the trip."

"It's lovely," Bessie said, sounding pleased. "I'll leave it out. Will you and Mister Donovan be working here tonight, Miss Rebel?"

"No. There's a board meeting. I'll probably be late, so don't wait up for me."

"Be sure you eat something," Bessie ordered tartly. "You're far too thin these days."

Thinking of the reflection she had just studied, Rebel silently agreed with her. "I'll eat. Did Donovan tell you to expect Dad? He's flying in tonight for the meeting and then going back to Paris and Mother tomorrow."

"Mister Donovan told me. Fine thing, your father flying all over the place at his age! You get him home at a decent hour, Miss Rebel, so he can get his rest."

"Dad and Mom enjoy travel, Bessie; you know that's why he retired early," Rebel said patiently. "But I'll try to get him home quickly. See you later."

"Take care," Bessie said automatically before hanging up.

Rebel sat back and stared at the phone, feeling an inexplicable sense of alarm. *Mister* Donovan. How long had Bessie called him that? The affectionate, semiformal address was her mark of approval—had been for years. She used it only with the family she'd been a part of for as long as Rebel could remember, the family and a very few select friends. And she didn't use it lightly; with Bessie, one had to earn respect and affection.

It was . . . funny. Even after nearly three years of marriage and numerous attempts on his part to charm her, Jud had never been called anything but Mr. Anderson. Rebel's husband had never won Bessie over.

Why did that make her suddenly uneasy?

She was tired, that was all. She was just tired, and that was why she was receiving all these crazy impressions and being attacked by ridiculous uncertainties. With a sigh and an effort, Rebel drew forward the agenda for that night's meeting and began to study it.

The Sinclair lawyers drew up the necessary documents giving Donovan power of attorney in the short time allowed. But what with one thing and another, the Sinclair company jet didn't leave the Dallas/Fort Worth airport until well after lunchtime the next day. She had had lunch with her father and Donovan, and she had been puzzled more than once by the former's unconcealed amusement.

Her father had seemed to think something was terribly humorous, but feeling a bit cramped by Donovan's presence, Rebel hadn't asked him what it was. She had a feeling, though, that it was the job-switch between her and her executive assistant, which she had told him about. He had, to Rebel's surprise, approved of the deception, but the laughter in his blue eyes had unnerved her for some reason.

Now, away from Dallas, the company, and her father, Rebel tried to relax in the comfortable lounge of the jet, but she found it impossible. She had unfastened her seat belt as soon as they had reached cruising altitude, and she shifted about restlessly. The luxurious cabin was silent except for the soft whisper of pages turning, and she sent a guarded glance across to Donovan.

He was apparently absorbed in the papers he had taken from his briefcase, his dark head bent and a slight frown between his slanted brows.

There had been half a dozen such trips in as many months, usually overnight whistle-stops at one or another of the Sinclair hotels, for reasons ranging from on-the-spot inspections to managerial meetings. On all such occasions, the journeys to and fro had been made in relative silence unless business matters had to be discussed.

For the first time, the silence bothered Rebel.

Body language, she thought vaguely, studying Donovan covertly. He looked indolent, slumping as though to disguise his great size. He gave the impression of a large, languid man of latent physical power and no more than average mental abilities.

The giveaway was his eyes. Although Rebel couldn't see them at the moment, she conjured in her mind's eye a vivid image with astonishing ease. She saw dark-fringed violet eyes, striking and startling and alive with intelligence. There was nothing lazy in those eyes, and certainly nothing stupid. Violet eyes with a dozen mysterious shades.

As if he sensed her steady regard, Donovan's eyes lifted suddenly to meet hers, and Rebel felt a sharp, physical jolt. Shock sent tingles all the way to her toes, and she wondered dimly what in heaven's name was wrong with her. There was nothing in his eyes to cause such a sensation, nothing unusual. Just a faint question.

"Is something wrong?" he asked quietly.

"No." But Rebel couldn't seem to look away, and

butterflies abruptly emerged from chrysalises inside her stomach and began fluttering madly. Odd . . . she had the absurd feeling that she'd never really looked at him before, never really seen him.

He stacked the papers neatly in his case and then got to his feet, returning her stare rather searchingly. "You look a little pale. Drink?"

She nodded slowly and watched while he made his way to the bar near the door leading to the cockpit. Automatically he began mixing her favorite drink, a screwdriver. Rebel wasn't really paying attention to his actions, though. She was busy having an attack of sheer panic.

Always mistrusting extremes in anything, Rebel had never been overly susceptible to masculine beauty. Her ex-husband had been an average man in looks, temperament, and intelligence. Other men she had been attracted to in her twenty-eight years had also been average, she reflected.

But Donovan Knight was not average. For one thing, the man was *big*. Close to six and a half feet, Rebel judged, and built on noble lines. He had shoulders that an all-pro tackle would have happily sacrificed his Superbowl ring for, a massive chest, and long, powerful arms and legs. Not a spare ounce of fat anywhere. He moved with the unthinking, sensuous grace of a stalking jungle creature. His voice was deep and resonant and almost incongruously soft for such a large man. His black hair was thick, and a little shaggy, and strikingly silvered at the temples.

And his face . . . his face was the closest thing to pure male beauty that Rebel had ever seen or imagined. Lean and strong, with high, well-molded cheekbones, straight dark brows, a finely chiseled aquiline nose, and a strong jawline suggesting a great deal of character. His curved, faintly amused-looking mouth possessed the odd trait of seeming to be both hard and soft at the same time.

Studying him in profile as he mixed the drinks, Rebel thought about that mouth in a crazily detached way. Hard, but not really, she decided finally. Softened by humor. Not a cynical humor, but a fun-loving humor—a humor that enjoyed life and people.

Rebel's panic returned. What was wrong with her? Why was she suddenly looking at Donovan in this entirely new and unwelcome way? Oh, this whole situation was going to become impossibly complicated.

Picking up the drinks from the bar, Donovan suddenly seemed to freeze, his head snapping around and startled violet eyes meeting hers. Rebel tried vainly to read the play of emotions across his face, but she captured only a few fleeting impressions. Astonishment, bemusement, uncertainty, faint shock. And then a curious sort of satisfaction.

What in the world—?

Donovan almost immediately thawed—or whatever—and came toward her with the drinks. He seemed undisturbed now by whatever had struck him. But there was a new expression in his veiled eyes.

Rebel was granted only a few seconds to try to read that expression, and it wasn't enough time. But she got the impression that he was suddenly pleased with something.

She controlled a start of surprise as he sat down beside her before handing her the screwdriver. She reached to accept the glass, uncomfortably aware that she was trying to avoid touching his fingers. But she did touch them—did he move them at the last minute?—and nearly dropped her glass. Hastily, she sipped the drink.

"This trip should be interesting," Donovan said, his voice just a shade more friendly—a shade more intimate?—than usual.

"Oh? Why is that?" she asked, knowing the answer.

"I get to boss around the boss-lady."

It wasn't so much what he said as how he said it that caused Rebel to turn her head and stare at him. "Looking forward to that, are you?"

"Sure. It's what every underling fantasizes about."

Rebel frowned at the term *underling* and then ignored it. "Why do you work for me?" she asked suddenly, honestly curious.

"Because I want to," he replied, unperturbed. An odd little smile curved his lips as she watched. "I have to work for someone."

"No." Rebel shook her head slowly. "I don't think you have to work *for* someone. Don't try to tell me you couldn't be your own boss if you wanted to. I assume you have to work, though; most of us do."

"You don't," he said coolly.

Rebel felt a surprisingly sharp stab of bitterness. She turned her attention back to her drink, her lips twisting slightly. "You mean the country-club route? Rich man's daughter, and all that? I've tried that, thanks. Never again."

"No, I can't see you spending your days playing tennis or golf and your nights attending boring parties," he agreed softly, something strangely intimate in his voice. "I'll bet it bored you silly."

"Something like that."

"So you divorced the man and married the company."

Rebel felt another jolt of surprise. How had he managed to associate her country-club days with her marriage to Jud? Her father hadn't told him; that wasn't Marc Sinclair's style. Still, gossip ran rampant in the company; perhaps he'd heard about it that way. She brushed the thought aside. "The company's less trouble," she said lightly.

He chuckled unexpectedly. "Easier to control, anyway."

For some reason his remark stung. "If you're implying that I have to dominate," she said defensively, glaring at her drink, "then you couldn't be more wrong."

"I didn't say that, boss."

Yet another jolt. He'd never called her that before. And why was it, she wondered desperately, that he said "boss" the way another man might have said "honey"?

"Then just what did you say?" she demanded.

"That a company's easier to control," he said patiently.

She darted a look at him, finding his face grave but his eyes twinkling slightly. Deciding that discretion was the better part of valor, she changed the subject. "I hope Lennox doesn't give us the runaround; we've wasted too much time in getting the land as it is."

Donovan followed the change of subject and then promptly gave it a new direction. "He should be reasonable about it. By the way, I should warn you about something. According to what I've heard, Lennox will automatically assume that you and I are having an affair."

Rebel choked on her drink and turned watering, disbelieving eyes to Donovan. After a moment she said with dangerous restraint, "That man should be stuffed and mounted as a relic of a bygone age! How in heaven's name did he reach his position in life believing such stupid, utterly ridiculous—"

Soothingly, Donovan murmured, "He inherited the money, the power, and the arrogance. I hear he always has affairs with his secretaries, including the present one."

Rebel wouldn't let herself be soothed. "I don't care about his sexual habits! I'll soon disabuse his mind of the idea that you and I are—"

"I wouldn't, if I were you," Donovan interrupted dryly. He went on in the same tone of voice when she gave him a glare. "He'll just assume that I'm stupid and that you're—excuse the expression; it isn't mine—fair game."

A militant spirit entered Rebel's heart. "I'll handle him," she said evenly, almost relishing the prospect. It occurred to her that tacking a "Mrs." onto her name might have discouraged groping hands, but she refused to consider it. Not even for the best of reasons could she pretend to be happily married while wearing Jud's name.

"I'm sure you know how." Apparently engrossed in a study of his brandy, Donovan missed the suspicious glance she threw him. "Better be prepared for a pass right off the bat, though. That dress you're wearing would arouse the hunting instinct in a cigar-store Indian."

In the act of raising her glass for another sip, Rebel froze and felt heat sweep up her throat. So he *had* noticed her change of appearance! The offhand compliment, though, gave her a sudden impulse to tug up the low V-neckline of her blue silk dress.

Not that she did, of course.

Still gazing at his brandy as though into a crystal ball, Donovan went on conversationally, "That hairstyle, too, is very sexy. Just a few strands to soften your face and the rest in a knot on top of your head. It gives a man an almost overpowering urge to take all the pins out and watch it cascade down you back in a shower of silver fire. Very sexy."

Rebel, the glass still frozen halfway to her lips, found herself staring at him and experiencing a profound sense of alarm. Was he still talking about Lennox? Somehow she didn't think he was.

She found herself listening silently to his drawling, resonant, musical voice, feeling hypnotized. Like a rabbit watching the hawk circling lazily above it.

"It's a curious thing about women. They often change their appearance abruptly for no apparent reason. But there's always a reason. Always. Maybe they get bored and just want a change. Or maybe it's some . . . outside influence, something someone else says or does. Or maybe it's the seasons. Hard to tell for sure."

Why had he changed the subject? Or had he?

"Anyway, you'd better watch Lennox." Donovan's voice remained in the low, pleasant drawl. "He thrives on pursuit. Would you like me to play knight-errant and chase him away? Warn him off? You know: 'She's not mine yet, but I'm working on it'?"

Rebel lowered her glass slowly, realizing that some-where along the way she'd lost her desire to "handle" Lennox. "Let's do whatever you think best. If Lennox believes I'm off-limits, maybe he'll concentrate on busi-ness."

"Whatever you say, boss."

Was there a quickly hidden gleam of satisfaction in his eyes? she wondered uneasily.

Donovan leaned forward to place his glass on a low table in front of them and then rose to his feet, casually patting her silk-covered knee along the way.

"I'll go talk to Buddy and find out when we'll arrive. Can I get you anything first?"

Highly conscious of her tingling knee, Rebel could only shake her head silently. She watched him lift a hand in a half-mocking salute and then move forward. Mo-ments later she was alone in the quiet, luxurious cabin.

Rebel lifted her own hand and methodically drained her glass of every last drop. There was a little gremlin in the back of her head whispering the unsettling con-viction that she should have remained in Dallas and al-lowed Donovan to perform this task solo.

Chapter **2**

REBEL SNUGGLED HER chin down into the fur collar of
her coat, jammed her cold hands a bit deeper into its
pockets, and sent a glowering look up at the equally
glowering sky. It looked like snow, she decided unhap-
pily. It looked like a *blizzard*. Any minute now.

For a brief moment, she flirted with the idea of buying
land from somebody other than Lennox. Anybody. Anybody, she amended silently, without prejudices against
female company presidents.

With another murderous glare at the leaden sky, Rebel
sighed and resolutely delved into the heart of the matter.
She was uneasy about this role-reversal business. Period.

It was fine to tell herself that it was just for the sake
of convenience and very temporary. It was also fine to

tell herself that the ploy was necessary in order to acquire that land. What was *not* fine was the inescapable knowledge that a ruthless man could easily take advantage of the situation.

And the sixty-four-thousand dollar question was: Was Donovan ruthless?

Until today, Rebel would have sworn that he was not. She would have said that Donovan Knight would put the interests of Sinclair Hotels above his own. She would have said that he was not interested in lining his own pockets. She would have said that he was not interested in taking advantage of the situation, or in stepping over the line that fate had drawn between them.

She would have said all of that. Until today.

Rebel looked around in an effort to rid herself of her unnerving thoughts. The airport runways stretched before her. It was as interesting as any other airport, which meant not very. And the view coming in on the jet had been daunting, to say the least. A native of Texas, she was used to flat land, but as much of Wyoming as she'd seen had looked like a flat, unfriendly desert.

Rebel stepped sideways to get the jet out of her line of sight and stared into the distance, where mountains reared to an imposing height. Snowcapped, some of them. Buddy had assured them that there had been "very little" snow this year and that the roads should be clear. Wonderful. They'd get there, but would they ever be able to leave?

Thinking about getting there spawned another thought, and Rebel cast an impatient glance toward the terminal. How long did it take to rent a car, for heaven's sake? Donovan was probably talking to a pretty clerk, and here his boss was, freezing her . . . The thought vanished into nothingness as a sleek new Mercedes pulled up on the tarmac beside the jet and Rebel.

"That doesn't look as though it can climb a mountain."

She directed her annoyed comment to Donovan as he got out of the car.

"Don't let looks deceive you." He was busy stowing their cases in the trunk.

Stubbornly, Rebel refused to let the subject drop. "Well, I hope you insured it; I'd hate to have to pay for that thing if a rock fell on it or something."

Donovan shut the trunk lid firmly and then cocked a knowing eyebrow in her direction. "Cold getting to you, boss? I told you to wait in the jet."

Rebel toyed with the idea of pulling rank, then discarded it. "It was stuffy in there," she muttered instead, and she was immediately alarmed to hear the defensive note in her voice. What was wrong with her? *She* was the boss, not he!

Donovan bounced the car keys a couple of times in the palm of one hand. "You or me?"

"You." Rebel sighed and headed for the passenger side. "I'm too depressed to drive." To her surprise, he came around to open the door for her.

"Why depressed?" Before she could either answer or get into the car, he added. "Better take off your coat; the heater's going full blast, and it's a good one."

Rebel would have preferred to leave the coat on, knowing that the wide fur lapels hid her low-cut dress, but she silently removed the garment and watched him toss it onto the back seat before getting into the car himself. And she didn't answer his question until he had slid behind the wheel. He had discarded his own coat, tossing it in the back with hers.

When Donovan started the car and drove toward an exit, she finally answered him. "Why should I be depressed? After all, I'm only leaving my home two weeks before Christmas to spend a lovely week or so in the back-of-beyond mountains of Wyoming with a man who has the mentality of a feudal lord and the hands

of an octopus." Taking a breath, she repeated sardonically, "Why should I be depressed?"

"I'm not that bad," Donovan murmured innocently.

"Funny man. I'm talking about Lennox, and you know
it."

"Well, I'll be there, too, you know. Any interesting
insights into *my* character?"

"You're a dark horse," Rebel answered promptly. She
shot a glance at his face. "And getting darker all the
time."

"And you should never bet on a dark horse, right?"
Donovan seemed to be paying attention to the traffic
leaving the airport.

Momentarily forgetting that they were talking about
personalities, Rebel answered automatically. "Oh, I don't
know. Dad always says that you should never count a
dark horse out of the running until it crosses the finish
line."

The Mercedes changed lanes smoothly, and Donovan
smiled oddly without looking at Rebel. "Thanks, boss.
You've given me hope."

Rebel feverishly cast about in her mind for a change
of topic. She didn't understand Donovan's remark—at
least, she hoped she didn't—but she didn't like it. Before
she could come up with anything, however, Donovan
changed the subject himself.

"Why 'Rebel'? I've always wondered."

She accepted the topic gracefully. At least it was better
than the other one! "Well, Dad's Irish and Mother's
German. Dad said that any child of that union was bound
to be a rebel."

Donovan chuckled. "That sounds like Marc."

"Uh-huh." She sighed. "He says he's just glad that I
didn't get his red hair."

"My mother says the same thing about me—that she's
glad I didn't get her red hair, I mean."

Rebel looked at him curiously. She was strongly aware that the conversation was on a more personal level than was customary between them. She knew that she should change the subject and avoid personalities, but curiosity won.

"Are both your parents living?" she asked.

He nodded, still paying attention to his driving. "In Virginia." While Rebel mentally gave herself high marks for perception and observation, he went on, "Like you, I'm an 'only'. Mother's been pestering me for years to marry and settle down."

Rebel hastily spoke. "Virginia's a long way from Texas. How did you wind up there?"

Donovan shrugged. "After college, I decided to see a bit of the world. I kept traveling, working as I went, until I ended up in Mexico, and then Texas. When I heard about the opening at Sinclair, I decided to settle down and try that for a while."

"Indefinitely?" Rebel asked dryly, registering that a lot of his knowledge of hotels probably came from the years of traveling.

"That wasn't my idea when I entered the building," he admitted cheerfully. "It was when I came out."

"I suppose Dad persuaded you?"

"Not exactly. You might say that I wished on a star. And, having wished, I had to stay until the wish came true."

Rebel had the confused desire to remind him that the interview with her father had been conducted in broad daylight, but she knew he had been speaking metaphorically. "What did you wish for?" she asked finally.

He sent her a reproachful glance. "You know better than that. If I told you, then the wish wouldn't come true."

"I never knew you were fanciful."

"There's a lot about me you don't know, boss."

Rebel sighed inwardly. He was right. And it made her nervous.

They left Casper far behind them, the silence in the car as companionable as could be expected. The mountains ahead of them loomed ever larger and ever closer and a few snowflakes drifted down lazily, unthreateningly.

When the Mercedes came to a stop some time later, Rebel tried to blink away the sleepiness born of inertia. "Why are we stopping? We haven't even started to climb yet."

Donovan was sitting with one arm over the steering wheel, smiling and obviously amused. "This is as far as the car can take us, I'm afraid. The last leg of our journey demands alternate transportation."

Short on sleep, unnerved and unhappy, Rebel wasn't disposed to humor. "First by jet, then by car—what's next? Don't tell me! We get into the nearest covered wagon, or climb onto a mule. Did you remember to pack the beads to soothe the natives with?"

He chuckled. "The natives are friendly. And the transportation isn't that primitive. Take a look."

Rebel's eyes followed his pointing finger. She craned her neck and looked, and then she looked again. When she spoke, her voice was deadly calm. "I'm not getting into one of those."

"It's the only way," Donovan said patiently.

Rebel ignored him. "We'll take the road."

"There *is* no road."

"There *has* to be a road. They couldn't have built a lodge up there without a road."

"Your needle's stuck," Donovan murmured, a slight tremor in his voice.

Rebel rounded on him with a glare. "You knew! You

knew all about this, didn't you? Why didn't you tell me?"

"You wouldn't have come," he replied simply.

She felt her heart give an ungentle lurch, and then she reminded herself that he needed information only she possessed about the proposed hotel. That was why he wanted her to come; that was why she was here. The thought fueled her anger.

"I will not get into a helicopter," she told him with careful restraint.

"You fly in the jet about once a month," Donovan said reasonably. "What's the difference?"

Rebel hated his rationality. Those things fly nose-down, and it makes me dizzy. I won't get into one. There must be a more civilized way to get to the lodge."

"The one I rented won't fly nose-down, and—"

"What do you mean the one you rented? Are you saying that that octopus-handed fuedal lord builds a lodge on top of a mountain and then makes his guests *rent* helicopters to get to him? Of all the— Do you remember the top price we're willing to pay for that land?"

"Of course I remember."

"Well, knock it down a thousand, dammit."

Donovan was openly grinning. "Right. If I can get a word in here, I wanted to tell you that there's no road. There *was* one when the lodge was built, but a rockslide destroyed it. Lennox decided to leave it as it was. And since it's a private road...well, call it a rich man's whim."

"Wonderful. And if a guest doesn't have the taxi fare?"

"Beats me, but he didn't offer to pay ours."

Rebel gritted her teeth. *"You* go. I'll go back to Casper."

"I'll need you here, and you know it."

"If he asks a question you can't answer, excuse yourself and find a phone. I'll be in that cute little motel next to the airport."

Donovan gave her a measuring look. "That's a very childish attitude, you know," he said conversationally.

Not at all offended or provoked, Rebel responded cordially, "I know—isn't it terrible? We all have our little fears, and that's mine."

"Why?"

"Why what?"

"Why are you afraid to fly in helicopters?"

"I can't be rational about it, for heaven's sake! I'm just afraid. I won't go, and that's final."

"You're just being stubborn."

"You bet I am."

"Rebel, it's a short flight. Ten, fifteen minutes. You can close your eyes."

"And what'll I do about my stomach?"

Donovan changed tactics. "Do you want that land?"

"Yes."

"Then you have to come with me."

"No. You can wing it—no pun intended."

"Rebel—"

"*No*. Donovan, I'm *not* going!"

"Rebel . . ."

It took nearly half an hour of patient arguing from Donovan before Rebel finally gave in. By that time she'd been backed into so many corners that she felt rather like a hunted animal. She was still arguing when Donovan calmly picked her up and set her on the back seat of the blue-and-white helicopter he'd managed to drag her to. He fastened her seat belt just as she was telling him in an aggrieved voice to be sure to call her father should she die of heart failure.

Donovan simply grinned and shut her door, climbing into the front beside the pilot.

Rebel realized two things in that moment: one, that he'd picked her up; two, that she was going up in this thing whether she liked it or not. Neither thought did anything to settle her nervous stomach or calm her disordered senses.

She promptly covered her eyes, silently berating herself for the phobia but not at all ashamed of it. As she'd told Donovan, everyone has some sort of fear.

She had been up in a helicopter one time in her life, and that had been one time too many. Surprisingly, though, she didn't feel all that frightened this time. Hesitantly, she parted the fingers covering her eyes and peeked between them. Not too bad, she decided a little sheepishly, as long as she watched the sky and ignored the ground rushing past below.

Donovan had half turned on his seat, watching her with a faint smile. When she finally dropped her hands into her lap, he told her, "See? It's not bad at all." He had to practically shout to be heard over the roar of the aircraft.

Irritated by his composure and her lack of it, Rebel yelled back rashly, "I'll get you for this!" She saw his lips move in a reply, and she blinked as he turned around again. Not that she was adept at reading lips, but hadn't he replied, "Oh, I hope so"? No . . . ridiculous.

They left the small heliport, with its rescue and private craft, far behind, and within moments were surrounded by imposing mountain ranges. Rebel didn't bother to look for signs of civilization, convinced that there weren't any. She didn't even look for Lennox's infamous retreat. She just stared at the back of Donovan's dark head and wished vaguely that she had a star to wish on.

Rebel was so wrapped up in her own muddled thoughts that when Donovan turned and gestured, it took her a moment to realize what he meant. She leaned forward and looked out the side. And her eyes remained glued

to the sight before her until the helicopter settled gently
on one of three concrete pads beside the lodge.

What had she expected? A lodge. Logs maybe, and
native rock. Rustic, cozy, practical. But this lodge was,
indeed, a rich man's whim. If Cinderella had been an
American story, this would have been the prince's castle.

It perched—literally—on the side of a mountain,
hosting the most spectacular view Rebel had ever seen.
Above it, its base mountain was snowcapped and majestic. Below it was a sheer drop, a couple of smaller mountains, and then the flat, desertlike plains of eastern
Wyoming. Aspen and pine covered the slopes.

The lodge itself was magnificent. No wonder guests
didn't complain about the taxi fare.

The wood was not rough-hewn logs but beautifully
weathered timber, and the native rock was plentiful. But
the rest was glass. There were huge windows on every
side, taking full advantage of the views. The central
structure was a tremendous A-frame, at least fifty feet
from base to apex, its multipaned glass front facing south-
east. Twin wings swept out to either side and ended in
smaller versions of the central A-frame. Behind the first
level was a second one, rising to follow the lay of the
land. It, too, held an A-frame, slightly off-center to the
left. A third level rose behind it, its A-frame off-center
and to the right.

How many rooms did it hold? Thirty? Fifty? Rebel's
opinion of Lennox—provided that he had guided the
architect—rose. This lodge wasn't just grandiose, it was
a perfect jewel in a perfect setting. And it was breath-
taking.

She accepted Donovan's help getting out of the helicopter, her eyes still fixed on the lodge. Moving to the
foot of the stone steps that led from the helipad to the
central A-frame, she finally turned away, shaking her
head, and watched Donovan get their cases out of the

aircraft. He talked briefly to the pilot and then joined Rebel at the steps, and both watched as the helicopter rose gracefully and soared away.

"Sure this is it?" Rebel asked dryly, gesturing with one thumb over her shoulder.

Facing the lodge, Donovan looked over her head to gaze up at it. He nodded. "This is it. Some altitude, too. Notice how thin the air is?"

"I noticed. If the helicopter ride didn't kill me, the lack of oxygen certainly will."

Donovan looked down at her and grinned. "You don't usually complain, boss. Something bothering you about this trip?" His eyes were wickedly innocent.

Rebel said the first thing that came into her head. "Look, an octopus is still an octopus, even if I do admire his house. I'm not exactly looking forward to this."

"I offered to assume the role of knight-errant," he reminded her. "Come to think of it, I'd probably enjoy the part; it's one I've never played. Shall I post a no-trespassing sign, boss?"

Rebel found herself staring at his mouth, and she hastily looked away. "It's freezing out here; let's go in."

He glanced over her head and up at the lodge again. "Someone's coming. I'm afraid I'll have to take the decision out of your hands. If I have to watch Lennox pawing you—or trying to—I'll probably knock him off his own mountain. Not good for business, boss."

"What—?" Rebel barely had time for the one strangled word before she found herself held securely against a massive chest. She could feel the powerful arms wrapped around her even through the thickness of her winter coat, and she wasn't sure if her breathlessness was due to the thin air, his sudden action, or her pounding heart.

"Donovan!"

"Command decision, boss," he murmured just before his head bent and his lips covered hers.

For a split second Rebel made no move either to push him away or to respond. She had a weird, distorted image of something crashing down within her, and she wondered idly if she was seeing her own defenses bite the dust. She found her fingers clutching the lapels of his coat, and she felt one of his hands coming up to cradle the back of her head.

After that, there was only sensation. He tasted of brandy and exuded a piny scent matching the mountain they stood on. Cold air blew all around them, bringing a needle-sharp awareness to Rebel's skin. She felt his mouth moving gently on hers, and she was aware of her lips blooming and warming in response.

Rebel heard him mutter something against her mouth, and she tried to make sense of the words. But then he was kissing her in a new way, a probing, demanding, devastatingly possessive way, and she forgot his attempt at speech.

She wasn't on the side of a mountain; she was at its top, and a giddy sense of vertigo swept through her. Clouds rushed past, billowing like sails in the wind. Her heart was pounding like a jungle drum gone mad. She thought that she was falling, but the fall was insidiously comforting, and she made no effort to save herself.

A sound intruded. Someone clearing his throat? But that was impossible; they were all alone on top of the moutain. It was absurd to think that anyone could get up here without wings.

She found herself staring blankly up at Donovan's face as he held her shoulders to put her gently away from him. His eyes, she noted dimly, were clouded, more deeply purple than she had ever seen them. He was breathing as roughly as she, and he shook his head slightly as if to clear it. Rebel was aware that her hands were still clutching his lapels, but she was unable to make them let go.

Rebel watched Donovan turn his head at last, apparently to greet the throat-clearer, and she heard a painfully British voice speak. "Good afternoon, Mr. Knight. Miss Anderson. I am Carson, Mr. Lennox's butler. If you'll follow me, please? I'll send someone down for your bags."

Emerging from her trance, Rebel looked at the butler with a flicker of interest. Where had Lennox found him? she wondered. The man had more dignity than Sinclair's entire board of directors. And his voice had been almost inhumanly devoid of expression, as was his face. He was as correctly attired as any butler would be expected to be . . . in a ducal mansion.

Donovan gently removed Rebel's clinging hands from his lapels and tucked one into the crook of his arm. "Carson." He nodded cheerfully. "Lead the way."

Halfway up the steps, Rebel realized abruptly that she was being awfully meek about all this, and belatedly she attempted to pull her hand from beneath Donovan's. His hand tightened to prevent the move, and she cast about in her mind for some suitably cutting remark. For Donovan's ears only, she hissed, "That was a wasted effort—for the butler!"

"Not at all," Donovan murmured in response. "Good practice."

Desperately certain that she'd made a total fool of herself by responding to his kiss, Rebel had a sudden impulse to push him down the steps. With any luck, he'd roll right off the mountain and she could avoid facing him.

"If you keep glowering," Donovan murmured, still not looking at her, "Lennox will think we've had a lover's spat and he'll try to catch you on the rebound."

Rebel wondered where she had lost control of this situation. When this loony idea had first popped into her head? When she had *seen* Donovan for the first time on the jet? When he'd managed to get her into a helicopter entirely against her will? When he'd kissed her with a hunger she didn't understand?

Oh, Lord...would this day never end?

The inside of the lodge was as manificent as the outside. It had been, Carson told them, dubbed Eagle's Nest by the workmen who had built it, and the name had stuck. Not very original, Rebel noted, but certainly appropriate.

It looked as if a decorator had been allowed free rein inside, given his head and an unlimited budget. The front doors opened into a great room, and it was entirely open from the plushly carpeted floor to the rafters—solid oak beams, from the looks of them—fifty feet above. The carpeting was off-white and ankle deep, the scattered chairs and couches a rust color and nearly as plush as the carpet. A tremendous fireplace graced the back end of the A-frame, occupying nearly the entire wall. Made of stone and beautifully crafted, it was large enough to roast a whole steer.

Carson gave them the grand tour—apparently the customary practice—and Rebel was exhausted when it was over. She had lost count of the rooms, and was bewildered by the number of dens, lounges, and living rooms. She also felt a bit dizzy at the decorating schemes, which changed from wing to wing. One modern, one Early American, one Louis XIV, and so on. And she had deduced early on that every stick of furniture and every bit of porcelain was a genuine whatever-it-was-supposed-to-be.

It wasn't until Carson was leading them toward their suite that Rebel noted two significant things. One was the conspicuous absence of their host, and the other was the dangerous word *suite*.

Wanting to put off the moment of confrontation with

Donovan as long as possible, Rebel hurried into speech as Carson was opening the door to their suite. "When do we meet our host, Carson?"

If Carson thought the question odd coming from the secretary rather than the boss, he didn't show it. "Mr. Lennox's apologies, Miss Anderson, but he was forced to fly to Denver on urgent business. He should return tomorrow afternoon, and he asked that you and Mr. Knight enjoy yourselves until he returns."

The butler related the information with a perfectly expressionless face, but Rebel read all sorts of hidden meanings into Lennox's message. She could easily imagine the leer that had probably accompanied it. And the hand still captured by Donovan's arm tightened in sheer temper.

She tried to remember how badly she wanted the land, but she knew she'd be hard put to keep from greeting Lennox with a haymaker he wouldn't soon forget!

Carson led them into the apartment, explaining that each suite had been designed with guests in mind and was made up of a sitting room, two bedrooms, and two baths—which relieved one of Rebel's cares. Their suite was at the front of the house and in the modern wing. The furniture was ultramodern but looked comfortable: a modular couch and a love seat of sorts, a couple of chairs, a desk in one corner. The floor was polished hardwood with rugs scattered here and there, including a white fluffy one in front of a huge fireplace. That rug, Rebel thought, positively invited one to sink bare toes into it.

The bedrooms, too, looked comfortable, although Rebel looked into hers only long enough to see that her luggage had been placed at the foot of the wide bed.

Carson told them when and where dinner would be served, pointed out the bell in the sitting room, which they could ring if they wanted anything, politely invited them to explore the house further if they wished, and then bowed himself out.

Rebel barely waited until the door clicked shut behind him before jerking away from Donovan. She took off her coat and tossed it at a chair, feeling her polite expression dissolve and the glower return. She wanted very badly to vent her confused emotions on somebody and Donovan made a large and inviting target. But he took the wind out of her sails.

"I know you're upset about what happened on the steps," he began directly, his coat joining Rebel's on the chair, "but surely you see that it's the best way. Lennox will concentrate on business, and you won't have to worry about being pulled into dark corners."

Momentarily deprived of ammunition, Rebel quickly made up the lack. "It was the *butler!* Would you like to tell me why the butler had to think we're having an affair?"

"It was good practice," he returned, unperturbed.

"You don't need any practice," she snapped. She immediately regretted the remark.

"Thank you," he murmured, a smile tugging at his lips.

Rebel crossed her arms defensively over her breasts and the low-cut dress. "I didn't mean it like that," she said in confusion, determined to get control of herself. She drew herself up to her full and usually imposing height of five eight and glared at him. "I don't like playing that kind of game," she announced coldly.

"Afraid?" he asked softly.

It was a direct challenge, and Rebel felt some of the steel melt from her spine. "Afraid of what?" she asked uneasily.

"Afraid of letting go of that strictly-business facade and allowing the real you to emerge?"

Rebel suspected that that was the point when she should call for a helicopter and leave without another word. But she knew for sure that Donovan was challenging her and that Marc Sinclair's daughter had never refused a challenge.

She lifted her chin and deepened the glare. "There's no 'facade' to let go of."

"Oh, no?" Donovan strolled over to one of the wide windows and gazed out at the spectacular view. Then he turned back to her and spoke calmly. "Rebel, you've wrapped Sinclair Corporation around you so tightly that it's like a chrysalis. If that's just a stage of development, then it's fine; butterflies emerge from chrysalises. But if you don't break out, then there's no development. No growth, no change. Just stagnation."

Rebel kept her voice level with an effort. "And you want to help me break out of the chrysalis, is that it?"

Donovan hesitated for a moment, his veiled eyes searching hers as though looking for something. Whatever it was, he apparently didn't find it, for his sigh held resignation. "You're going to take this the wrong way, but yes, I'd like to help you do that."

"Gee, thanks." Rebel didn't know what other way she could have taken it. "To what do I owe the honor?"

He sighed again and leaned a hip against the desk by the window. "Don't lose your temper, please. I'm not talking about our so-called affair. I'm talking about the fact that you've forgotten how to relate to someone on a one-to-one level. You look at people, boss, as though you're sizing them up across a bargaining table. With you, it's always black or white—no shades of gray."

"Anything else?" she asked tightly.

"Yes," he answered levelly. "There is one other thing. Your appearance. Over the past year, I've watched you strip yourself of layer after layer of feminity. Your hairstyles became more severe; you cut your nails and stopped polishing them; your suits became more formal, more masculine. No jewelry, no ruffles or frills. Even your walk changed, became brisk and businesslike. You've become a caricature of a businesswoman."

Rebel felt a chill as he echoed her thoughts of the day before. Before she could speak, he was going on.

"Until today. Today you look very feminine, very sexy, and very much a woman. Today you look like a business*woman,* rather than a *business*woman. You're breaking out of that chrysalis—or trying to."

Mercifully, Rebel thought, he didn't speculate on the reasons for her change. "I want to be taken seriously," she defended herself, troubled to realize that she had taken that idea to its farthest extreme.

Donovan shook his head. "You're respected for what's inside, Rebel, not what's outside. Your first duty is to gain the attention of whomever you're dealing with. So why not use the ammunition God gave you?"

Rebel wanted to consider that a sexist remark, but somehow she didn't think it was. She met his eyes, noticed the searching expression in them, and strove to keep her own blank.

After a long, silent moment, Donovan sighed. "Look, forget the business angle for the moment. According to Marc, you haven't had a vacation since you left college, and that's been three years. Until Lennox gets here, why don't we both relax and consider this a brief vacation? It won't hurt, and it'll probably do us both good."

Rebel nodded slowly, thoughts of her "chrysalis" flitting through her mind. Had it really gotten that bad?

"Good." Donovan's voice was unusually gentle, as though he saw or sensed her weary confusion. "Now, why don't you lie down and try to rest before dinner? It's been a long day."

Silently, Rebel turned and went into her bedroom, closing the door behind her. She told herself that she was only agreeing to his suggestion because she was tired.

But the real reason was that she had felt tears sting her eyes suddenly. Inexplicable tears. And she didn't want Donovan asking questions that she couldn't answer.

Chapter 3

DINNER WAS A strange affair. It was as if, Rebel thought, she and Donovan were strangers. Careful, tentative questions elicited guarded answers. The company wasn't mentioned, nor the reason that had brought them to Wyoming. They tacitly avoided potentially dangerous topics, falling back on the trite and commonplace.

Carson—white gloves and all—served them in a dining room that could have seated twenty people without crowding. The pheasant was delicious, as was the remainder of the meal. But Rebel, desperately aware of the deteriorating conversation, hardly noticed. She finally excused herself before Donovan could resort to polite conjecture about the Superbowl this season.

She found her way into the central greatroom and sat

down in a chair near the fireplace, watching flames lick at what looked like half an oak tree. Moments later she nearly jumped out of her skin when large hands came to rest on her shoulders.

"You're as tense as a drawn bow," Donovan said quietly from behind her chair. His fingers began to move in a gentle, soothing massage. "Relax."

Rebel wanted to tell him that it was impossible to relax with him touching her, however innocently, but she managed to bite back the words. She couldn't, however, halt the sensations rushing through her body. The warmth of his hands easily penetrated the thin silk of her dress, setting her nerve endings on fire. Her heart was pounding, and she felt again the dizzying sense of vertigo. What was the man—a warlock? Why did he make her feel this way? She had never felt this way before, not even with Jud. And she'd *loved* Jud. Once, she had loved him. Before she found out...

Donovan spoke again, quietly, calmly, cutting into her thoughts. "You know, of course, that I want you."

Rebel stiffened and stared blindly into the fire. "Do you?" She was amazed that her voice was so calm.

"Very much."

"You never mentioned it before," she observed, for all the world as though they were talking about something unimportant.

"You never looked at me before. Not the way you've been looking at me today."

"You're imagining things," she scoffed.

"No. Until today you had never really seen me as a man, had you, Rebel?"

Rebel shifted uneasily and found that his hands, gentle though they were, would not let her escape. She wondered suddenly why he was standing behind her. The thought had barely crossed her mind when he came around the chair, drawing forward a hassock and sitting down to face her. Deliberately or not, he had chosen a position that made it impossible for her to get away.

"You've been so wrapped up in that damned company that you never noticed anything else—until today."

"How you do harp on this supposed tranformation of mine," she managed lightly.

His jaw tightened—the first sign of temper she had ever seen in him. "Rebel, don't try to avoid the issue."

"And just what is the issue?" she asked evenly.

"Us. And what we could have together."

Rebel didn't like the question that was plodding with deadly slowness, deadly clarity, through her mind. But it was there, and it hurt her in a way she hadn't been hurt in years.

What was Donovan really after—her, or Sinclair Hotels?

If she asked him, he'd only deny any interest in the company, she thought cynically. But Rebel strongly mistrusted his sudden interest in her as a woman. So . . . what? A confrontation now was the last thing she needed or wanted.

"Oh, damn," she murmured at last. "I forgot the key."

Donovan blinked. "Key? What key?"

"The key to my chastity belt."

Looking for the effect of her soft words, Rebel watched as Donovan leaned back slightly and stared at her. Somewhat to her surprise, he didn't become angry with her flippancy, but instead seemed thoughtful. After a moment, he nodded slightly as though coming to a silent decision. And when he spoke, his voice was as light as hers had been.

"We could always call a good locksmith."

"Wouldn't work; the belt's an old model."

"At least a few years old," he murmured innocently.

Rebel started to snap at him, and then remembered that she was supposed to be taking this whole conversation lightly. "At least," she agreed limpidly.

It was Donovan's move, and she waited to see if he would at least try for a stalemate. But Donovan neatly retired from the board, and Rebel didn't know whether to be relieved or disappointed.

"Ah, well, forgive the trespass, milady. I'm abashed."

"A bashed what?"

"Cute. Is that what they call rapier wit?"

"It's what they call tired wit. If you'll kindly get out of my way, I'll go to bed."

Donovan got to his feet and politely moved aside so that she could rise. He made no move to follow her, and he didn't speak again until she was at the archway leading to their wing.

"Fair warning," he said cheerfully. "I'm very adept at picking locks."

Rebel turned to look at him. "I'll just bet you are," she deadpanned. "So—fair warning to you: This lock's booby-trapped."

Donovan inclined his head slightly at the warning. "Good night, boss," he said, his cheerfulness not diminished by one iota.

"Good night."

Rebel managed to find her way to their suite—no mean feat considering that she wasn't really paying attention to where she was going. Going through the sitting room, she noted that someone had built a fire in the fireplace, and she wondered if Carson believed the night would be filled with romancing. Shoving that curiously painful thought aside, she went into her bedroom.

The busy "someone" had turned down the quilted spread on her bed and laid out a peach satin nightgown. Rebel methodically got ready for bed, her blank mind a result of weariness rather than effort. As she slid between cool sheets and reached to turn out the lamp on her nightstand, she wondered how on earth she was supposed to sleep . . .

Rebel didn't remember closing her eyes, but when she opened them light was flooding the room. She lay there for a moment and blinked at the ceiling before sitting up.

The events of yesterday rushed through her mind in a kaleidoscope of impressions, ending at last at the semiconfrontation of the night before. She'd been wrong, Rebel realized now, in believing that Donovan had retired from the board, conceding defeat. He had merely retreated to a tactical holding position.

So whose move was it now?

Shaking off the question, Rebel slid from the bed. A glance at her watch on the nightstand told her that it was nine A.M., which meant that she'd slept nearly eleven hours. No wonder she felt rested! During the past few years she'd averaged no more than six or seven hours of sleep a night.

Now she felt wide awake, clear headed, and ravenous. Probably the mountain air was responsible for the last, she thought.

Since her cases had been unpacked the day before, Rebel searched through drawers until she had the clothing she wanted. She told herself fiercely that Donovan's comments had nothing to do with her decision to put the businesswoman away in her briefcase for a while. She told herself that . . . but she didn't believe herself.

In the bathroom, she resisted the invitation of the sunken tub large enough to host an elephant, opting instead for a quick shower. Some time later she stood in front of the full-length mirror in the bathroom and stared at her reflection critically.

Apparently Donovan had told Bessie to pack some

casual clothes, because the jeans were certainly not something Bessie would have automatically included. Faded and growing shiny in the seat, they hugged her slender hips and thighs. She had chosen a blue cowl-necked sweater to go with the jeans. It was bulky, but not so much so that it hid the curves beneath. After a brief struggle with herself, she put up her hair in a casual, girlish ponytail, trying to ignore an urge to leave it down and see if Donovan said anything. She had applied her makeup carefully and deliberately, and now she studied the overall effect.

She looked years younger and not in the least like her mental image of a businesswoman.

Smiling with satisfaction, Rebel returned to her bedroom and searched for shoes. She found scuffed riding boots and lifted her eyebrows briefly in silent surprise, then shrugged and pulled on the boots. At that moment she would have bet half her company that there were horses somewhere about.

Leaving her bedroom and going through the sitting room, she glanced into Donovan's room and saw the bed neatly made and very empty. That didn't surprise her; she would have bet the other half of her company that he was an early riser.

Rebel took her time finding the dining room, partly because she got lost and partly because she wanted to explore some more anyway. She wandered from wing to wing, gazing at furnishings and decorations and becoming increasingly puzzled. One room in particular—in the Early American wing—disturbed her. There was a rectangular spot on one wall that indicated that a large painting was missing, and that bothered her, although she couldn't have said exactly why.

She was gazing at the bare patch on the papered wall when she became aware that she was no longer alone. Turning slowly, she felt her eyes widen in surprise.

At first guess, it was at least half timber wolf. A closer look told Rebel that she was staring at one of the largest specimens of Siberian husky she had ever seen. And the ice-blue eyes were narrowed and suspicious.

Rebel didn't waste any time. With a dog of that size, the smart thing would be to become friends as quickly as possible. She dropped down to her knees and held out one hand, palm down. "Hello, fella. Where did you come from?"

The husky advanced, bit stiff-legged, and examined the hand held out to it. A sniff, and then the curled tail wagged tentatively. Within moments, the big dog was practically sitting in Rebel's lap and busily washing her face with a tongue the size of a hand towel.

Rebel held on to the thick silver-gray ruff of the dog's neck and giggled as she tried to save her makeup. "Stop that! I won't have a face left when you get through."

"I see you've met Tosh."

She jumped to her feet as the dog abandoned her to dash to the large form leaning against the doorjamb. Watching the dog frisking around Donovan's feet, Rebel mentally discarded the formality she'd planned on assuming today. It didn't fit her new image, and besides, she didn't need formality as a shield. Did she?

"He's beautiful. Why didn't we see him yesterday?"

Donovan bent slightly to scratch a blissful Tosh behind one ear. "Carson said he was at the stables."

Rebel silently gave herself a gold star for intuition and studied Donovan while he was paying attention to Tosh. He was dressed more casually than she'd ever seen him, in jeans and a ski sweater. Like her, he was wearing boots. He looked relaxed and cheerful, and for the first time, she noticed the laugh lines at the corners of his eyes.

When he looked up and met her gaze, Rebel said the first thing that came into her head. "I wonder why that painting's missing," she murmured, jerking a thumb over her shoulder.

Donovan looked at the naked wall and then shrugged. "Ask Lennox, if he ever gets here."

Rebel felt a sense of foreboding. "What do you mean if he ever gets here?"

"You didn't look out your window this morning, did you?"

"No." Rebel frowned. "Why?"

"We had a little snow during the night. Denver had more than a little."

"Lennox isn't coming?"

"Not today. I just talked to him on the phone. Apparently Denver is snowed in. Doesn't happen often, but it does happen."

Rebel sighed. "Uh-huh. It figures."

"Cheer up," he directed lightly. "We get another day of vacation. Now, how about breakfast? Then we can saddle up and explore some of the trails around here."

"In the snow?"

"Why not? The horses are used to it."

"How do you know I can ride?" she challenged.

"That picture Marc used to keep on his desk," Donovan supplied instantly. "I think you were about sixteen and had just won some kind of rodeo final."

Rebel felt a twinge of pain as she remembered those carefree days. How long had it been since she'd ridden? Not since the divorce. Seven years. Where had the time gone?

"Hey." Donovan had crossed the room to stand in front of her. "Sorry if I struck a nerve; I didn't mean to."

"You didn't." She stared fixedly at some point near the middle of his chest.

"No?" His hand lifted to firmly tip her chin up. "Then why do you look so sad?"

Gazing into his quiet, curiously shuttered violet eyes,

Rebel felt suddenly that she could tell him this, that he would understand. She couldn't remember the last time she'd confided her feelings to anyone, and she wondered dimly if she'd really lost touch with other people so completely.

"Tell me," he urged softly.

She uttered a shaky laugh. "For a minute there—when you mentioned that picture on Dad's desk—I felt old. And I wondered what had happened . . . and why it happened so fast."

The hand beneath her chin shifted to gently cup the side of her neck. "And you felt lost and alone," he finished quietly.

Rebel nodded mutely.

Donovan drew her into his arms and held her firmly, resting his chin on the top of her head. "It happens sometimes," he said pensively. "Odd moments when everything screeches to a stop and you wonder where the time has gone. You wonder if you've made a wrong turn somewhere, and what would have happened if you'd turned left instead of right."

He *did* understand, and Rebel let herself relax in his comforting embrace. "It's a scary feeling," she whispered.

"Very," he agreed. "But don't let it throw you, boss. I won't let you get lost for long, and you're never alone."

Rebel carefully stepped back, vaguely disappointed when he made no effort to stop her, and stared at him. "Why am I never alone?"

"Because you've got me." The words were uttered lightly, and he immediately took her arm and began leading her from the room. "I'm your man, boss. Always have been. Ready for breakfast?"

Breakfast was a lighthearted meal, thanks largely to Tosh, who begged shamelessly for bacon. Thanks also to Donovan, who kept up a steady flow of utterly mean-ingless, totally absurd conversation.

"Did you know that there's a legend about an old prospector who climbed this mountain and never came down?"

"Is there?"

"Yes."

"And so?"

"And so what?"

"Is there a point to the story?"

"Not really."

"Then why did you bring it up?"

"Seemed the thing to do."

"I'm going to dock your pay."

"Ssshh—Carson will hear you."

"I don't care."

"You should. There's another story—"

"I don't want to hear it, Donovan."

"—about a mermaid who lives in a cave near here."

"Mermaids live in the ocean."

"This one lives in a cave."

"Yeah? How do you know?"

"Carson unbent enough to tell me about it."

Rebel casually slipped a piece of bacon under the table for Tosh. "Unbent? He'd have to un*ravel* to tell you something like that."

"Stop feeding the dog; he's half grizzly bear already."

"Who's feeding the dog?"

"You are. That's the third piece of bacon you've snuck to him."

"You're seeing things."

"And you're going to split hell wide open if you keep lying like that."

"You're playing Russian roulette with your future, buddy."

Donovan shook his head, blatantly feeding Tosh a

piece of bacon. "I know. My boss is a holy terror. No sense of humor."

"Your boss is currently having her ankle chewed on by half a grizzly bear. What did you do, drop that bacon on my foot?"

"Tosh, stop that!"

"Forget it. I'll just have to buy a new pair of boots."

"Speaking of boots, are we going riding or aren't we?"

"You just want to see me suffer, don't you?"

"It's been a while, huh? Since you've ridden, I mean."

"A while," she agreed wryly. "Seven years. An hour in the saddle, and I'll be sore tomorrow."

"I'll ask Carson for some liniment and give you a good massage. How's that sound?"

It took Rebel a moment or so to remember that she wasn't going to take him seriously. Just the thought of his hands on her bare body was enough to send a flame through her veins. "Thanks, but I think I can handle it," she managed at last.

"Spoilsport."

"That's me. Shall we head for the stables?"

Donovan didn't appear at all downcast by her offhand rejection. "After you, boss."

"As it should be."

"Why?"

"Because if you go first, nobody sees me."

"There's nobody here to see either of us."

"It's the principle of the thing."

"Oh."

With a laugh, Rebel serenely preceded him to the door, halting only long enough to don a thick flannel jacket that Donovan pulled from a closet.

"How did you know that was there?"

"Carson."

That figured. "Whose is it?"

"Beats me." Donovan pulled another jacket from the

closet and put it on. "This one's mine," he said before she could ask. "I left if here earlier this morning."

Rebel accepted the information. He could hardly have pulled a jacket from the closet that just happened to fit him; his size wasn't exactly average.

He led her unerringly from the lodge to the stables along an almost invisible path. Their boots crunched in the two or three inches of snow, and a slight cold breeze blew all around them. The morning was pleasantly brisk; in fact, it made Rebel feel very alive.

The stables were tucked away beneath trees and on the gentle slope of the mountain, built on levels like the lodge. There were roughly twenty separate stalls opening into various wide halls, a feed room, and a tack room. And two horses were tied near the tack room, saddled up and ready to go.

"You called ahead?"

"Came down this morning. The palomino's yours; her name is Sugarfoot."

Rebel reached to stroke the mare's golden neck and then tugged at the snowy white mane. "Lennox sure does himself proud," she murmured almost to herself. "This has to be more than just a lodge. I've counted four stable hands; the house staff is made up of Carson, a house-keeper, four maids, and a cook; and there are twenty horses here. Not to mention Tosh. He keeps all this on tap just for vacations? Doesn't make sense."

"It does if you're rich apparently. Want a leg up?"

"No, thanks." Rebel untied Sugarfoot, glancing over at the big muscled bay gelding Donovan was preparing to mount. "Does he have a name?" she asked, swinging into the saddle lightly.

Donovan grinned at her as the horses moved out of the wide hall. "Sure. His name's Diablo."

Rebel couldn't bring herself to comment, but it struck

her as vaguely unnerving that Donovan was riding a horse named Devil.

Their ride lasted for nearly two hours and covered several different trails, including one that passed by a hollowed-out place in the side of the mountain that could have been taken for a cave.

"Told you there was a cave."

"Where's the mermaid?"

"She must be hibernating."

"Cute."

Beginning to feel chilled and definitely stiff, Rebel gratefully accepted Donovan's suggestion that she dismount at the lodge and let him take the horses back to the stables. She felt long-unused muscles protest as she swung down, and she winced slightly as she stepped over to hand Donovan the reins.

"I think you've killed me, and all for nothing. I didn't leave you a thing in my will," she told him darkly.

He chuckled. "You'll recover. I'd advise a hot bath."

"I'm way ahead of you. Don't fall off the mountain on your trip down to the stables."

"Concerned, boss?"

"Dreadfully. You have to be alive to keep me from killing Lennox when he finally arrives."

"Is that all I'm good for?" he asked, wounded.

"Don't ask loaded questions. 'Bye." Rebel turned away and headed for the door. She passed two of the maids and Carson on her way through the house, and she wondered again about Lennox's lodge.

Something about this whole place bothered her, but she just couldn't pin it down. She probably could have pinned it down, she realized wryly, if only her mind would assume its normal habit of working properly. But she'd been off balance and rattled since this trip had begun. And she had a sneaking suspicion that this state of affairs was entirely due to the sudden change in her relationship with Donovan.

In her bathroom, Rebel located bubble bath provided by her thoughtful and still-absent host, poured it into the huge sunken tub, and then rapidly stripped while the tub was filling.

At all costs, she thought, she had to avoid a confrontation with Donovan over what he was really after. A confrontation would ultimately end in one of two ways: Either she would fire Donovan, or he would quit—neither of which would do. She told herself that her concern was because of the land; she needed Donovan to bargain with Lennox.

For the first time, Sinclair Hotels felt like an albatross around her neck. No, not for the first time. But for the first time in years. And this time it hurt terribly to understand that she could well be only the means to an end—the end of controlling a vast and profitable corporation.

Shoving the thoughts into the small and rapidly overflowing room in her mind reserved for "tomorrow," Rebel wound her ponytail into a knot on top of her head, stuck a few pins in it, and climbed into the tub.

She turned off the taps and leaned back in the hot water, letting the bubbles and the heat pamper her. The tub was deep, and the bubbles reached nearly to her chin.

The thoughts in their little room continued to tease her, and Rebel finally gave up the attempt to ignore them. They wouldn't wait for tomorrow. She admitted to herself, silently and painfully, that Donovan's "I want you" had stirred something inside her. If she had felt nothing, the possibility that he was after the company would not have bothered her, would not have hurt.

But it did bother her; it did hurt. For the first time since the divorce, she was interested—no, fascinated— by a man. Setting aside their roles as employer and employee, could she have any sort of relationship with a man whose eyes were fixed on the president's chair? The nontraditional roles didn't really bother her, and she didn't think they bothered Donovan either—although that was easy to say here, far away from the office.

No, the real question was what Donovan wanted. If it was the company, no relationship was even conceivable. But if he wanted just her, well...Rebel closed her eyes and let herself think about what that might mean.

A sharp knock sounded on the bathroom door, followed by a cheerful, "Are you decent?" and just barely preceded by Donovan's entrance into the room.

Rebel instinctively grabbed a woefully small washcloth and held it to her breasts, covering what the dissolving bubbles were beginning to expose. Caught totally off guard, she stared at him in speechless indignation.

Dressed only in jeans, which left bare an unexpectedly furry chest, Donovan casually perched on the raised edge of the tub and gazed down at her. His eyes flitted briefly over white flesh visible between disappearing bubbles and then swiftly returned to her flushing face. And Rebel had the odd feeling that he was holding on to some private resolution with both hands.

"Cocoa." He held out a large mug. "To warm up the inside."

"I don't like cocoa!" she snapped. "Leave!"

"You could at least be polite," he observed reprovingly.

"To a man who charges unannounced into my bathroom? Not bloody likely! Take your cocoa and leave!"

Donovan set the mug down on the tiled floor. "I thought I'd wash your back for you."

Rebel felt her heart bump against one hand. She tried desperately to assume the boardroom dignity she'd acquired over the years, but she found that dissolving bubbles and a half-naked man did nothing to promote any kind of dignity at all. The assurance of twenty-eight years and a corporate presidency notwithstanding, she had never felt more vulnerable in her life.

"Leave," she whispered finally. "Donovan, please leave."

His violet eyes were slowly darkening to purple. "You don't really want me to go." He leaned forward to press his lips briefly to one soapy shoulder. "Do you?"

"I don't want things to change," she managed, not even sure what she meant by that.

"Things have already changed." One of his hands had cupped the back of her neck, and he was drawing her slowly toward him. "You can't turn back the clock. It might not have happened except for this trip, but it did happen. Nothing will ever be the same between us, Rebel. Not now. And you know that as well as I do."

Rebel watched his face coming closer, lost herself somehow in the depths of his purple eyes, and a last protest died in her throat.

When his lips touched hers, she felt something flare inside her, something primitive and hungry. One of her hands abandoned the cloth she was still holding against her breasts to touch his lean cheek with a need beyond thought, beyond reason. Her lips parted willingly, eagerly, beneath his.

Donovan explored her mouth slowly, as though all the time in the world was theirs. He defied any resistence, seduced and defeated it. She could feel tension in him, and a burning heat, and she realized dimly that he was holding himself rigidly in check.

Rebel couldn't believe that she could be so deeply affected by a simple kiss. Every nerve ending in her body came vividly alive, throbbing with feelings and sensations she had never known before. The warm water flowed all around her; his fingers brushed lightly, gently, against the side of her neck; his lips held hers like an insidious trap made of satin. Colors whirled behind her closed eyelids—reds and purples and sparks of silver fire. Tension grew in her like a living thing.

And when his lips finally, abruptly, left hers, Rebel wanted to scream aloud in frustration and disappointment. But she didn't make a sound; she simply blinked up at the man who had risen and was now towering above her.

Donovan murmured something beneath his breath and shook his head slightly, a gesture she remembered from the day before and that electrifying kiss at the bottom of the steps. When he spoke, his voice was only a shade more hoarse than usual.

"Lunch will be ready in half an hour. I'll meet you in the dining room. Okay?" He barely waited for her silent nod before leaving the room.

Rebel tried to think clearly, tried to make her mind work in its usual shrewd and logical manner, but to no avail. Only one thing kept revolving in her head. What he had said beneath his breath a moment ago, what he had muttered against her mouth yesterday at the bottom of the steps.

"A year," he had muttered hoarsely. "My God . . . a year . . ."

Chapter 4

ONCE AGAIN, REBEL decided to treat her relationship with Donovan lightly. It would not be easy, she knew, because Donovan had made the next move. He had made it clear to her that role-reversals and a pretense of knight-errantry notwithstanding, he wanted her.

And Rebel had realized when Donovan had left her alone with her bubbles that she wanted him as well. Had that been his intention? The soul-destroying kiss ending abruptly and leaving her unsatisfied? Perhaps. If so, then she could expect other interludes calculated to wear down her resistance.

Her resistance . . . oh, that was funny. If Donovan only knew, her resistance to him was absolutely nil. And that was why she had to keep things light between them.

Because if she didn't—if she turned left instead of right and jumped blindly into a serious relationship—then she would never be able to be sure that it was her and not the company that Donovan wanted. And that would blast her self-respect, leaving it as tattered as her marriage had.

So Rebel slowly and carefully got a grip on her bewildered senses as she climbed from the tub, dried off, and dressed. She used every mental trick she had ever learned, pouncing on traitorous desires and wrestling them into sheltered corners of herself. She did not examine her own feelings, flinching away as one would to protect a raw wound. She simply repressed them.

She dressed in slacks and a light sweater, thoroughly brushed her hair, and refastened it into the casual ponytail. Then she composed her face into calmness and headed for the dining room.

One of the many phones throughout the lodge was in the dining room, and Donovan was talking on it when Rebel entered. She was too preoccupied to listen closely to what he was saying for a moment or so, merely noting silently that he had donned a Western-style flannel shirt over the jeans and reclaimed his boots. She also noticed that his black hair was damp from a recent shower, and she felt a flicker of interested speculation as to whether it had been hot or cold.

Then she pushed aside the thought and stared at his broad back, his end of the conversation breaking through her abstraction.

"...and one day more or less *will* matter. Because the timing has to be perfect, that's why. No. No, blindly unsuspecting. What do you mean sudden? It's not sudden at all. Never mind that now; I'll explain later. Just do it." His level voice roughened suddenly. "I don't care if it upsets airline schedules all over the world; this is important to me!"

He was silent for a few moments, apparently listening to the person on the other end of the line. "All right, then. No, he's still in Denver. Well, it's obvious, isn't it? Wouldn't you smell a rat? Right. I'll make the arrangements. See you then."

As Donovan replaced the receiver, he stiffened suddenly and then turned slowly to meet Rebel's watchful gaze. He looked startled and ill at ease for a split second, and her suspicions climbed a good three or four notches.

"Who was that?" she asked mildly.

Donovan slid his hands into the back pockets of his jeans, matching her own stance, and seemed to brace his shoulders. "Josh—from the office."

"I know who Josh is, Donovan."

"Sorry."

"Well?"

Donovan sighed. "I talked to Lennox again a few minutes ago, and I think he's decided to play hard to get. He claims that an emergency business meeting has postponed his return to the lodge indefinitely."

Rebel's vague suspicions dissipated, and she felt herself beginning to do a slow burn. "Dammit! Then we'll go back to Dallas and look for another piece of property—"

"I have a better idea."

She studied him curiously. He appeared a bit diffident, and she wondered if that was why he'd looked uncomfortable when he'd turned and seen her listening to the conversation. Was he worried about taking the initiative?

"What have you been up to, Donovan?"

He grinned slightly, a wicked twinkle in his violet eyes. "I'll have to ask you to trust me on that point. Let's just say that I think I can get Lennox here by the first of the week—and he'll be more than willing to talk business. Nothing illegal," he added hastily. "Just a bit underhanded. And since we're already being slightly underhanded, I didn't think you'd mind if I... upped the ante?"

Rebel had a burning curiosity to know exactly what Donovan had planned, but something stopped her from asking the question, and she didn't know why. "All right. But I'll expect to hear the whole story before this is over with, Donovan."

"Oh, you will, boss. You certainly will."

During the light lunch of soup and salad, which followed hard on the heels of their conversation, Rebel reflected that this new turn of events meant at least four more days alone with Donovan. Of course, she could have flown back to Casper and then on to Dallas until Lennox was due to arrive here. But that would have entailed a sinful waste of the Lear's expensive fuel. No, she would remain here.

But her often-repeated resolution to treat her changing relationship with Donovan lightly would be sorely tested. Was, in fact, being tested right now. His new and disturbing way of looking at her—born on the jet coming out here—had increased in intensity. The warmth in his eyes was decidedly unsettling.

Her one serious romantic relationship had not prepared her for this man who looked at her as though she were an oasis come upon suddenly in a bleak and barren desert. A part of her wanted to give up and give in, to explore the possibilities and the promises she could see in his eyes. Another part of her resisted the urge, unable to bear the thought of laying what she was at his feet and watching him walk over her as Jud had. She wouldn't go through that again.

Rebel managed to make it through the afternoon, primarily because Donovan seemed bent on keeping her relaxed and amused. He unearthed a Monopoly game shortly after lunch and engaged her in a life-and-death battle on the floor of the central greatroom. Tosh lay before the roaring fire, wagging his tail from time to time.

"You cheated!"

"That's slander."

"So sue me, but move that piece back."

"Command order, boss?"

"You'd better believe it. Ha! I own that property—pay up."

"All right, but I'll have my revenge. See? That puts you in jail. Now who's one-up?"

"Don't gloat; it isn't becoming."

"You gloated when *I* landed in jail."

"That was different."

"Uh-huh. Want to buy your way out, jailbird?"

"Stop waving that card under my nose! All right, let's bargain. What do you want for it?"

"The key."

"What key?"

"How soon we forget. The key to the chastity belt."

"Too steep. Try again."

"No way. The key or nothing."

"Look, it's snowing."

"Stop avoiding the subject. The key."

"I'll give you all my property on that side of the board. Total control for you. How about it?"

"Nope. The key."

"Forget it, chum. The lady of the castle takes a dim view of someone else's holding her key."

"What about the lord of the castle?"

"There isn't one. He was pinching the maids, and I kicked him out. I can run the castle very nicely on my own, thank you."

"The jousting tournaments must be hell."

"Funny."

"The dragon-fighting, too."

"*Will* you be businesslike?"

"Knight-errants are romantic, not businesslike."

"Well, knight-errants don't own keys to chastity belts. It's a rule. They just borrow them."

"Oh. Can I do that?"

"No. Look what happened to Launcelot."

"Unlucky devil, wasn't he?"

"What do you expect? He tampered with the king's lady."

"Tampered. That's a new description."

"Don't be crass. How much for the card?"

"No key, huh?"

"Nope."

"Then let's try the barter system. Knights are good at that. I'll trade you this little card for another piece of paper."

"How many dollar signs are on that paper?"

"Just a couple."

"You want two bucks for the card?"

"No. I want a small piece of paper that *costs* two bucks—or thereabouts."

"You've lost me. What's this paper?"

"It's called a marriage license."

"Sorry. Not an even trade."

"You want out of jail, don't you?"

"Not that badly."

"Ouch. That hurt."

"Good. A hundred bucks for the card?"

"Plus the property?"

"Yes, dammit."

"Deal. If I can't have what I want, I'll take what I can. You're a shrewd businesswoman, boss."

"Right. I just lost control of one whole side of the board. My father would have a heart attack if he knew."

"You kept the key, though."

"Of course."

"And left a poor knight to eat his heart out."

Rebel began to soulfully hum the theme from *Gone with the Wind,* and Donovan threw a little red house at her.

"Frankly, my dear—"

"Don't say it!" she begged, laughing.

"—I think we should finish the game."

Sadly Rebel observed, "It wouldn't work without the moustache, anyway."

"Roll the dice, Scarlett."

The game was temporarily interrupted by dinner, the passage of time surprising both of them, but was picked up almost immediately after the roast chicken was demolished. Treading softly, Carson came into the greatroom once to build up the fire and was nearly out of the room before Rebel saw him.

"Carson, arrest Mr. Knight—he's cheating!"

"Sorry, Miss—this isn't my jurisdiction."

Rebel looked blankly at Donovan when the butler had gone. "Did Carson make a joke?"

"I think so."

"I wonder if he meant to?"

"Beats me. Are you going to put a hotel on Park Place?"

"It takes nerve to ask me a question like that."

"I beg your pardon, I'm sure."

Rebel finally called a halt to the game some time later, saying virtuously that she would no longer do business with an out-and-out shyster. Donovan looked so wounded that she nearly giggled, but she managed to keep a straight face as she wandered over to browse through a magazine rack. Donovan put away the board and the game pieces, then stretched out on a couch with a sigh of contentment.

"This is the life," he murmured.

"Don't get used to it," she warned wryly, locating a

fashion magazine presumably left by one of Lennox's lady friends. Deciding to get back in touch with current styles, Rebel took the magazine to a chair and curled up to study it. Both she and Donovan had shed their heavy boots right after dinner, and it was easy to get comfortable.

Physically. Mentally was another matter. Rebel quickly discovered that without the light banter that had been the rule for the afternoon, she had entirely too much time to think—and not about fashion.

She blanked her mind and flipped listlessly through the magazine, then set it aside on an end table. She found both her glances and thoughts straying to Donovan's apparently sleeping form, and she grew steadily more restless. The silence was unnerving.

Rebel got to her feet with the idea of turning on the extensive stereo system in one corner of the room. She needed background noise. Badly.

"In the cabinet by the left speaker," Donovan murmured.

Rebel froze and turned slowly to gaze at him, puzzled. He was lying with his eyes closed. "What?"

"The tapes. They're in the cabinet beside the left speaker."

"How did you—?" Rebel stared at him blankly.

Donovan's eyes opened abruptly and lifted to her, a startled, bemused expression flickering in their violet depths. "Oh...well, you looked as if you wanted to hear some music."

"I did?"

"Sure."

Rebel wondered briefly what her I-want-to-hear-some-music expression looked like, and then she realized something. "You weren't looking at me," she pointed out.

"Of course I was. How else would I know what your face looked like?"

That made sense. Rebel shrugged and went over to the stereo. It only took a few moments for her to figure the thing out. She chose a tape at random and pulled it from its slot, not even bothering to see what it was before she placed it in the player and flipped a switch. Immediately, loud music filled the room.

She hastily turned down the volume, inwardly cursing and horribly embarrassed. And not because of the volume.

Brilliant move! she silently and caustically applauded herself. Lennox probably kept this particular tape for the purpose of seducing his secretaries. It was Ravel's "Bolero." In Rebel's opinion, it was the most erotic piece of music ever written.

The heavy, sensuous rhythm filled the room even at low volume. She didn't dare snatch the tape from the player, knowing that her reason for the move would be easily understood. Instead, she wandered with apparent aimlessness toward the fireplace, hoping that Donovan would attribute the pink in her cheeks to the heat of the fire. She felt uncomfortable and unnerved, and her heart was beginning to match the beat of the music.

She wished that Tosh hadn't left with Carson; she could have made a fuss over him and maybe drowned out the damned music. Unfortunately, she and Donovan were alone.

"Lovely music," he murmured from the couch.

Rebel stared determinedly into the fire. "Lovely."

His next words came from right beside her. "Dance with me."

"You can't dance to this music," she objected quickly.

"Want to bet?" He took her hands and placed them at the nape of his neck, placing his own hands at her waist and drawing her close. Then he began moving. Slowly, sensuously, following the music.

Rebel kept her gaze fixed on his chin and attempted to keep a respectable distance between them. But his hands slid down to her hips, pulling her closer until their lower bodies nearly merged. Fiercely, she tried to ignore the sensations that caused.

"Do you know," he murmured conversationally, "that you're a beautiful, brilliant, incredibly exciting woman?"

It took all the willpower at Rebel's command to return a light, bantering response. "Be still, my heart."

He grinned. "Flattery doesn't move you, does it?"

"Not an inch."

"How about truth?"

"Truth is nice. I have a fondness for truth."

"Okay. You're a beautiful, brilliant, incredibly exciting woman."

"That's still flattery. Spanish coin."

"No. Truth."

"Gilded truth. You have a silver tongue."

"Really?"

"Oh, yes."

He was looking down at her with a sleepy sort of smile, eyelids heavy and lips just faintly curved. Lazy. And deceptive. Because she could *feel* the wide-awake awareness behind the sleepy look. And she wondered suddenly how she had ever managed to underrate this man to the point of not even seeing him.

"Who did this to you, Rebel?" he asked very quietly.

She blinked at him, startled. "Did what?"

"Battered your self-respect. Wounded the woman in you until she curled up and hid herself away. Damn near destroyed you. Who was it, Rebel? Your ex-husband?"

Rebel stiffened and tried to pull away, but he held her firmly, moving slowly to the heavy beat of the music. He continued to speak in a drawling, thoughtful voice.

"Oh, you're good at keeping things light. You didn't even turn a hair when I mentioned marriage. You're quick and you're witty, and you pass off everything as a joke." One hand slid up her back and began toying with her ponytail. "But there's no joke in your eyes. So tell me, Rebel. How badly did he hurt you? Was he a rotten husband?"

Rebel felt her lips twist into a bitter smile, heard her voice answer his question, and wondered why she was telling him this. "Oh, he was the perfect husband. Charming, attentive, romantic. Flowers for no special occasion. Little gifts on my pillow. We played tennis and golf and rode horses. We went to parties and out to dinner, and had marvelous vacations." She felt her smile harden. "And he satisfied me in bed. Anything else you want to know?"

Donovan's jaw tightened. His eyes had totally lost the sleepy look now and were reflecting what he saw in her eyes: something diamond-hard and painful. And the expression beneath the reflection of hers was searching, sober. "Were there other women?"

"Not that I know of," she responded brightly.

His hands gripped her shoulders. They had stopped dancing; neither of them was paying attention now to the music that throbbed seductively. "Why did your marriage break up, Rebel? Why did you divorce your husband?"

"Because it wasn't real!" she cried. She flung off his hands and turned aside trying to control herself and keep the bitter words inside. "I . . . don't want to talk about it, Donovan. Just let it drop."

"I won't do that, Rebel. I can't do that." He caught her hand, preventing her from escaping him. "You've kept this inside you for too long. Even your father doesn't know the whole story, and he—"

"My father?" She stared at Donovan, incredulous, furious. "You discussed me with my father?"

Donovan released a short, impatient sigh. "No, I didn't discuss you with him. I asked Marc a few questions, Rebel. Because I wondered what kind of bastard could destroy a woman the way that ex-husband of yours obviously destroyed you. But Marc didn't know what had happened. The only thing he was sure of was that you'd left your husband after less than three years and filed for divorce. You wouldn't talk to him, your mother, or Bessie about it."

"You had no business discussing me," she shot back tautly, tenaciously holding on to a subject less painful than her marriage. But she sent a silent thanks to her father. He'd known why her marriage dissolved; he had known long before she why Jud married her.

Donovan ignored the red herring. "Rebel, you have to talk about it. It's been eating away at you for years! Until you get it out of your system once and for all, you'll never be able to shed that chrysalis. You'll be just the shell that he left you with and nothing more! *Tell me.*"

"No!" Vainly, she fought to free her hand, finding it trapped in a gentle vise. "It's none of your business—"

"It *is* my business! Dammit, Rebel, what do you think I've been trying to get through to you since we got here? I want to become a part of your life, and that means knowing where the shadows are. How can I fight something I can't even see? How can I prove to you that you're a beautiful, desirable woman when I don't know what your ex-husband did to destroy your confidence in yourself?"

Rebel was still struggling vainly, forgetting dignity. She was trying desperately to avoid talking about what had happened, because it hurt now as it hadn't hurt in years. The confrontation she had wanted to avoid at all costs was here, and it hurt because she didn't know what Donovan wanted—her or the company.

"Rebel, tell me!"

"No!" She was utterly dumbfounded when she burst into tears. Dimly aware of his arms holding her, of her face pressed against his flannel shirt, she realized that it was the first time she'd cried since childhood. She hadn't shed a tear after leaving Jud. Dry-eyed and hollow, she'd simply picked up the threads of her life and gone on.

But she was crying now.

Donovan picked her up, holding her as easily as he would a child. He carried her to the couch and sat down with her in his lap. She could feel the tenderness in him, and somehow it made her cry harder. And the crooning, wordless sound of his voice pulled tears from wells she hadn't known existed.

It was a long time before she finally stopped, drained and weary. Donovan produced a handkerchief and dried her cheeks, then held the cloth and gently ordered her to blow her nose. Meekly, Rebel did as he commanded. Even in her emotional state she was conscious of the absurdity of the situation.

"Some boss I am," she sniffed woefully.

"You're a terrific boss." He held her firmly when she would have removed herself from his lap. "No man could have a better one. Now tell me why it wasn't real."

Rebel didn't have to ask what he meant. The music had ended, the player automatically shutting itself off, and when she spoke her voice was the only sound in the room other than the pop and crackle of the fire.

"It wasn't real because it wasn't. None of it was real. The charm, the attentiveness, the romance. The love he was so good at voicing—and making. It was fake, phony . . . a sham. All of it."

"Start at the beginning," Donovan urged quietly.

Rebel sighed and sniffed one last time. She felt small and vulnerable, and there was a dull ache inside her. Perhaps the tears had blunted the pain; she didn't know.

"I was eighteen and had just started college. I met Jud at a party. He . . . he made me feel special right away. He was charming and attentive, and he made me laugh. We spent almost all of our time together during the next two weeks. And then we eloped."

She laughed harshly. "Eighteen! What do you know about love at eighteen? But you're so sure. I don't think you can ever be as sure of love as you are at eighteen. Nothing else matters, nothing else is important. Just starry-eyed dreams."

Donovan tightened his arms around her slightly. "Go on."

"I dropped out of school, and we set up housekeeping. Dad gave us a house as a wedding present. I didn't think anything of it then. Jud had taken a business degree in college, but he earned his living as . . . as a tennis instructor." She flung back her head almost defiantly, expecting to see scorn or contempt in Donovan's violet eyes. But only gentle understanding met her searching gaze as he waited for her to go on with her story.

With an effort, Rebel swallowed the lump in her throat. "I knew Dad didn't approve, but he never said a word against Jud. He only wanted me to be happy, and if Jud could do that . . . well, he was willing to wait and see.

"It was a country-club life-style. We played tennis or golf during the day and went to parties at night. We had a maid—courtesy of Daddy—and two cars and a poodle." Rebel became aware that she had reverted to childhood's use of "Daddy."

"Jud didn't make very much money at this job, but I had an allowance and charge cards. We spent money like it was water, buying things we didn't really want or need on the spur of the moment."

"When did things start to go wrong?" Donovan asked softly.

Rebel shook her head. "That's the whole point: Things *didn't* start to go wrong. I mean, it wasn't a gradual thing. I was so completely and utterly blind that I didn't suspect anything.

"I thought that I had the most perfect husband in the world. I knew that he loved me as much as I loved him. There were no fights—not even small disagreements. I should have suspected something when I realized that; two different people can't live together every day without some disagreements, some . . . adjustments. But Jud made sure that the water was always smooth.

"It wasn't a marriage at all. It was just a play staged for my benefit. Oh, Jud said all the right words and made all the right moves . . . and it was all cold-bloodedly planned."

"How did you find that out?" Donovan asked.

"Brutally," Rebel answered shakily. "I was supposed to meet Jud for lunch, and I stopped by the office to see Daddy, since we hadn't talked in a couple of weeks. The outer office was empty; the secretary had already gone to lunch. I started to open the door to Daddy's office, and I heard Jud's voice."

Rebel closed her eyes and tried to forget the words she had heard that day. But her memory was cruelly accurate, every word and nuance of voice etched in her mind like neon.

"You'll never run this company, Anderson—I'll see to that!"

"Why else do you think I married your daughter, old man? Rebel does what I tell her to, and when you're gone, the company's mine."

"Rebel?"

She opened her eyes to see Donovan's anxious expression, his violet eyes worried as he tipped her chin up firmly and stared at her. "What did you hear?"

"Jud and Daddy were arguing," she replied flatly. "Jud was saying that Daddy should retire and leave the company to him. He said he'd get it anyway, once Daddy was gone. That he'd only married me for the company."

"Bastard!" Donovan muttered roughly.

Rebel barely heard him. In a toneless, faraway voice, she went on. "I've never heard Daddy so furious. Jud was jeering and confident, and Daddy was shouting that if I was hurt Jud would have him to answer to. Jud just laughed. He asked Daddy if he really thought I'd believe anything against him. He said that he—that he'd done his work well, that I'd never guessed the truth."

Donovan swore softly, roughly, one large hand cradling the side of her face. "The man was a fool, Rebel," he told her insistently, his voice still rough. "He didn't know—didn't have the sense to know—that companies are as common as flies, but a woman like you is one in a million!"

Rebel managed a watery smile. "Gee," she murmured.

He smiled tightly. "I mean it, dammit! He was an idiot, and I'd feel sorry for him except that I'd dearly love to break him into a few thousand pieces."

Her smile died a weary, painful death. Donovan went very still, something savage flaring in his eyes. The thought of what Jud had done chilled her, and she wanted desperately to be held tightly, comfortingly. To her vague surprise, Donovan immediately pulled her closer, wrapping his big arms around her in a warm bear hug. Her cheek was resting against the flannel covering his broad shoulder, and she could feel his chin moving gently against her forehead.

"What did you do, Rebel?"

She sighed raggedly. "I walked for hours after I left the office. I was numb. Stupidly, I finally thought that maybe I had misunderstood somehow. So I went home.

He was waiting for me, supposedly worried because I'd missed our lunch date. I confronted him with what I'd heard."

She was silent for a long moment, then shook her head slightly. "I should have remembered that Jud was a sore loser. He was always very even-tempered, except when he lost. At a game, or something small and petty. He'd blow up. I should have remembered that."

"Did he hurt you?" Donovan asked gratingly.

Rebel felt the words rushing from her, and knew that Donovan had been right; she'd held it inside for far too long.

"Not in any physical way. At first, he tried to deny it. But I could see the deceit in his eyes, and I knew he was lying. When he realized that I meant to leave him, he became cold and cruel. He . . . said things. Things that sickened me," she finished starkly. She was shivering now, in spite of the arms holding her close.

Donovan's arms tightened convulsively. "Forget what I said about feeling sorry for that bastard. If I ever come face to face with him, I'll kill him." His voice was flat and deadly.

Rebel lifted her head to look at him uncertainly. She saw pain in the violet eyes. Pain for her, she realized. Rage for her. It moved her oddly, and she had to swallow hard before she could tie up the loose ends.

"He stormed out afterward. I packed a few things and went to a motel. I stayed there for a few days until I could face things. I never told anyone what had happened. I just said the marriage was over and filed for divorce. Jud didn't fight me. I think he was afraid of Daddy. Anyway, it—it ended."

"Did it?" Donovan asked quietly.

Rebel looked at him and knew what he meant. It hadn't ended. Not really. She was still carrying the emotional scars from what had happened that day. And her response to Donovan proved that Jud's form of brutality had not destroyed her ability to feel desire. She was not afraid of men because of him.

But she was afraid of being a woman. Afraid to trust her instincts. Her self-confidence had never recovered from the blow Jud had dealt it.

Chapter 5

AFTER A LONG moment, Donovan sighed softly. "You think I might be after the company. That's it, isn't it?"

Rebel dropped her eyes to stare at the hands gripped tightly together in her lap. "I don't know what I think," she said dully.

"But you aren't . . . afraid of me, are you?" There was a thread of anxiety in his voice.

Rebel felt a flush rise in her cheeks. "No," she whispered. "No, I'm not afraid of you." She felt a sigh of relief from him.

"You're just afraid that I have my eye on the president's chair," he said finally.

She stirred uneasily but remained silent.

"Rebel, there's no way I can convince you. I could

tell you that I don't give a damn about the company except about how it affects you, but I can't prove that. I could promise to stay totally away from the office, find a job somewhere else, but I happen to enjoy working with you."

He laughed shortly, a bitter humor in the sound. "I sure picked some shadow to box, didn't I? Even now that I know what it is, I can't really fight it."

Rebel stole a glance at his face, bewildered by the urgency in his deep voice. What did he want from her? What part did he want to play in her life? And why did she want suddenly, desperately, to believe that he had no overwhelming interest in the company?

"It's up to you, Rebel," he said soberly. "You have to decide for yourself what kind of man I am. You're not eighteen anymore; you have more experience in judging people."

Rebel had nearly forgotten that she was still sitting in his lap. He was still holding her, comfortingly and undemandingly, and that was soothing her and making her feel oddly cherished. She hung on to the feeling, trying to work through the dilemma in her mind.

"It happened so fast," she murmured at last. "One moment you were the perfect assistant, and the next . . . the next, I didn't know what you were."

"I was slightly insane," he said dryly. "And after a year, I think I had a perfect right to be."

She looked at him hesitantly, remembering that he'd muttered something about a year twice after kissing her. "A year?"

"Uh-huh." His tone was wryly self-mocking. "You were the star I wished on, Rebel—a year ago. Remember that first day, when we ran into one another in the hall outside your father's office?"

"I remember."

"Well, that's why I hired on with Sinclair. After seeing

you, I was damn well going to stick around for a while. It didn't take me two seconds to realize that you were wrapped up in the business, but I figured you'd have to come out of it sooner or later. And I wanted to be around when that happened."

Rebel had a small feeling that her mouth was open, and she hastily closed it. "You mean you—you took the job just because you wanted *me?*"

"I've always been impulsive," he drawled consideringly.

His eyes were veiled, oddly watchful, and that suddenly made Rebel very nervous. She didn't know him. How many times had she looked at him unexpectedly and seen that expression in his eyes? Waiting, searching, watchful. She had noticed it only in passing, abstractedly, indifferently. His eyes were always quickly shuttered again, and she had dismissed the look. But now she wondered what lay behind it.

"Rebel, stop it!" His hands cupped her face, and his eyes were no longer veiled but dark and troubled. "Don't look at me as though you're afraid of me, honey. It hurts."

"What do you want from me?" she asked in a whisper, trying to ignore the bump her heart had given at the endearment.

He hesitated, a flicker of indecision showing on his face. Then he sighed roughly. "The hell of it is," he muttered, "that I've waited a long time to answer that question, and now I know damn well you won't believe me."

Rebel was trying to understand what he meant by that when he pulled her forward abruptly and kissed her. His lips were warm, demanding, and achingly hungry. He kissed her as though it were the last thing he would ever be able to do in this life—a final, desperate action before oblivion.

And she couldn't help but respond to that. Her mouth opened willingly beneath his, her hands lifted to tangle in the dark, thick hair at his collar. She could feel and sense the passion in him, the thread of restraint stretched nearly to the breaking point, and a part of her wished that it would snap. She didn't want to have to think . . . only to feel. And what Donovan made her feel was astonishing and strangely addictive.

His hands moved caressingly over her back, pulling her nearer and nearer until her breasts were crushed against the hard wall of his chest. She felt them swell and harden even through the clothing separating her flesh from his, and she heard a groan rumble from the depths of Donovan's throat.

When he finally tore his mouth from hers, it was with an obvious effort. A heavy shudder shook his strong body, and his breath came raspingly.

Rebel was left staring at him, her lips hot and throbbing, her heart pounding crazily. When she'd finally gotten her own breath back, she said shakily, "I guess that answers my question."

He shook his head slightly, the violet eyes slowly clearing. "Not entirely." His voice was hoarse. "Oh, I'm not about to deny that I want you. I'd have to be blind, stupid, or made of stone not to, and I'm certainly none of those. What we have together is magic, Rebel, but I want more than that."

"What—" she had to clear her throat before the words would emerge properly—"what do you want?" Her arms were still around his neck, her fingers still tangled in his hair.

"I want your trust, Rebel. Your trust, and your faith, and your heart. I want your love."

When the steady words finally sunk into Rebel's brain, she could only shake her head miserably. "You want too much," she whispered raggedly, feeling tired and confused and terribly afraid to probe her reaction to his words. "Even if I wanted to, I—I can't give you what I don't have to give."

"You're coming out of the chrysalis," he responded softly. "And that's a big move. Today—in spite of your trying to keep things light—you were more relaxed than I've ever seen you. And you laughed. Do you know that I'd never heard you really laugh until we came on this trip? And now you've told me something you've never told anyone else. Don't you realize that you had to trust me a great deal just to do that? I'm willing to build on it, Rebel. If you'll let me."

"Are you saying that you . . . that you—"

"That I love you?" His voice deepened, taking on colors and shades filled with meaning. "I think I've loved you ever since we bumped into each other in that hall-way."

Rebel wanted to believe him. Something inside her urged her to believe him. But the suspicious little gremlin born of Jud's deception jeered at her. She shook her head silently, numbed and bewildered by the conflicting emotions of the past hours.

After a moment, Donovan rose to his feet as easily as if he weren't holding a grown woman in his arms. He made his way toward the archway leading to their wing. "I think you need to sleep on it," he told her gently. "And I," he added with a sigh, "need to take a long walk in the snow."

She was too tired to make sense of the remark. "In the snow? But it's freezing out there." Fascinated, she watched a muscle tighten in his lean cheek.

In a very dry voice, he responded, "Honey, you're looking at a man who's holding on to his willpower with both hands and his teeth. Believe me, I need to walk in the snow for a while."

"Oh." Rebel hastily tucked her chin in and tried to

control the flush rising in her cheeks. It occurred to her that she should be making some protest over the fact that he was carrying her, but for the moment it was comforting to be carried like a child.

Donovan whisked her into their dimly lit sitting room and then through to her bedroom. He set her gently on the foot of the bed, grimacing slightly at the sight of her peach satin gown shimmering in the lamplight beside her. Quickly, he bent to give her an almost brutally short kiss.

"Good night, honey. Sleep well."

Rebel waited until he was at the door. "Donovan?"

He half turned to look back at her, and she could have sworn that he stiffened. "What is it, honey?"

She swallowed, the gremlin keeping back the words she wanted to say. "Be careful when you go out."

"Bet on it," he said lightly. He left the room, closing the door quietly.

Rebel stared at the door for a long moment, hearing the sitting room door shut, and then silence. She got up and automatically undressed, donning the peach gown before sliding between the sheets and turning off her lamp.

She had looked at the luminous dial of her watch twice, and an hour passed before she heard the quiet sounds of Donovan returning. Only then did she let herself slip into sleep.

When Rebel was awakened the next morning by a steady thumping sound, her first thought was that she'd certainly had peculiar dreams. Castles and jousting knights and golden keys dangling enticingly from turrets. Enticingly? Odd. Definitely odd.

The thumping sound connected itself to knocking in her mind just as Donovan poked his head through the door.

"Hey, sleepyhead, want to go look for Christmas trees?"

He was disgustingly bright-eyed and bushy-tailed, and Rebel glared at him for a moment before making an attempt to rub the sleep from her eyes. She had the irritating feeling that there was something she should remember, but it remained just out of reach.

"Christmas trees?" she responded grumpily, raising herself on her elbows, the better to see Donovan. "Can't Lennox find his own trees? There's a mountain full of them."

"Carson suggested it. I think his British soul is offended by the lack of ornamentation about the place. Want to help me repair the lack?"

Rebel smothered a yawn with one hand. "Can we have breakfast first?" she asked plaintively.

"Certainly. It's ready when you are, love."

The "love" triggered Rebel's memory, and her eyes widened as the events of the day before rushed through her mind. Given half a chance, she would have pulled the covers over her head and attempted to hibernate until spring.

"Don't panic on me, now," Donovan ordered lightly, apparently rooted in the doorway. "Today's just for fun— I promise. No serious discussions about anything. Are you game?"

Rebel found herself nodding in what she knew to be a very weak way. "I'm game," she murmured wryly.

"Then get a move on, milady—the forest awaits," he informed her cheerfully before leaving her alone with her muddled thoughts.

The forest awaits. Uh-huh. With her luck it would turn out to be an enchanted forest.

Sighing, Rebel pulled herself from the bed. It was better, she decided, not to think. She'd just take the days one at a time and try to get to know this impossibly large man who said he was in love with her. And maybe somewhere along the way she'd figure out what her own confused emotions were.

Donovan was as good as his word. A day for fun.

After breakfast, they bundled up in coats, scarves, and gloves burgled from various closets and they tramped over a winding trail to what Donovan said was the tree farm.

The tree farm turned out to be on a gentle slope some distance from the stables. A number of unhappy-looking stumps were mute testimony to this field's having been victim to Christmas-tree hunting for some years, but a larger number of seedlings also gave evidence of great care to replace what was taken. Spruce and cedar were the rule, with sizes ranging from the seedlings to one sixty-foot giant. Snow made a four-inch thick pristine blanket beneath the trees and provided a lovely contrast to the various shades of green.

Rebel had tucked her hair beneath a wool cap, and now she turned up her collar to ward off a blast of cold air. "You dragged me out of bed for this?" she grumbled once they stood in the center of the tree farm.

"Let's hear some Christmas spirit," Donovan chided.

"Bah humbug," she muttered.

"The ghost of Christmas past'll get you for that. Pick a tree, boss—for the central greatroom."

"What are you going to cut it down with—your teeth?"

"That's all taken care of. Pick a tree."

"Decorations?"

"Carson's digging them out now. Are you going to pick a tree?"

"Don't snap at me. I was just asking."

"I didn't snap at you, but I'm going to turn you over my knee if you don't get busy."

"You and what army?" she challenged huffily.

Donovan's violet eyes gleamed impossibly brilliantly

in the bright reflection of sunlight off snow as he grinned. "Don't push me, boss," he warned gruffly.

Rebel hastily went tree hunting. Trying to ignore the fact that Donovan was dogging her footsteps, hands in his pockets and whistling cheerfully, she finally picked a tree. It was a beautifully shaped ten-foot specimen. "This one."

Donovan studied it. "Nope. Too small."

She went looking again, and this time found a lovely fifteen-foot tree. "This?"

"Too small."

The next one was twenty feet. "Well?"

"Too small."

"Donovan, if you want a redwood, we'll have to go to California."

Ignoring her sarcasm, he turned in a slow circle, surveying the trees. Then he pointed. "That one."

Rebel stared at the majestic, thirty-foot cedar expressionlessly. "Shall I yell for Paul Bunyan?" she asked finally.

"Why?"

"Because we'll need his ax to cut that thing down, and his ox to drag it back to the lodge."

"Funny." He pulled a roll of bright red tape from a pocket. "Be a good girl and mark the tree. At the base there, high enough to see."

"Who's the boss here?" she wanted to know.

"I think we're still jockeying for position," Donovan said wryly.

Prudently not rising to the bait, Rebel silently marked the tree. When she had done so, she returned to Donovan and handed him the tape. "Why did I mark that tree?" she asked politely.

"So the men can find it. The stable hands are going to cut the trees for us."

"*Trees?* More than one?"

"Several." Donovan began ticking off rooms on his fingers. "This one's for the central greatroom. Then there are the two front dens, three lounges, the butler's pantry—"

Rebel was shaking her head. "Never mind. Just let me know when we're through. Are you sure there are enough decorations for all those trees?"

"Carson says so."

"Won't Lennox feel offended if we do this?"

"Do you care?" Donovan asked cheerfully.

Rebel thought it over. "Not really. However, I draw the line at decorating all these trees. It would take a week."

"Okay. Then we'll just decorate the one in the central greatroom and leave the rest to the staff. How's that?"

"Fine. But I feel sorry for poor Santa."

"Why?"

"All the chimneys at the lodge."

"We'll leave out a glass of brandy so he can refresh himself."

"I sincerely hope we won't even *be* here. And what kind of man would try and get Santa drunk?"

"Not drunk. Just pleasantly warm."

"Uh-huh. You pick the next tree."

The morning flew past as they argued the merits of each tree selected. Most of the trees were on the large side, but the one Rebel fell in love with was just barely six feet tall. A misguided bird had built a small nest among the needles and then abandoned it, and that lonely little nest touched something in Rebel. She didn't say anything about it to Donovan, but she thought more than once of suggesting that they select a tree for their sitting room. *That* tree.

She didn't, though.

After lunch, they repaired to the greatroom, where

the stablehands had managed to set up the thirty-foot cedar far enough from the fireplace to be safe. Boxes of decorations, strings of lights, and tinsel were grouped about at its base.

Rebel tucked a strand of silver-blond hair behind one ear and sighed as she surveyed the Herculean task before them. "How did I let you talk me into this?" she asked mournfully.

"My fatal charm," Donovan answered, busily engaged in untangling a string of lights that had probably been packed away neatly but had mysteriously tangled during the preceding year.

"Right." She hastily grabbed a handful of silver fur. "Tosh! Stay out of the tinsel, dummy. No, I don't want to play catch, and that isn't a ball! Lie down over there like a good boy."

"*Your* fatal charm," Donovan observed as the big husky obediently stretched out in front of the fireplace.

"Tosh knows the voice of authority when he hears it," Rebel said disdainfully. "Which is more than I can say for certain other members of this household."

"Has Carson been disobeying your orders, boss?" Donovan asked innocently.

"You know very well whom I meant. And how you've got the gall to call me 'boss' is beyond me!" she told him sternly.

"Well, because I'm yours to command," he replied, wounded.

"Then go find a ladder. Unless you plan to sprout wings and fly to the top of this tree."

"Yes, ma'am. Right away, ma'am." Donovan pulled an imaginary forelock and bowed with mock awkwardness several times until Rebel threw a plastic angel at him.

Tosh happily retrieved the angel, thinking that they

were going to play catch after all. By the time Rebel managed to wrestle it away from him, Donovan was back with the ladder.

Rebel made one attempt to climb the ladder and got dizzy halfway up, so it was left to Donovan—loudly gloating—to string the lights.

He gloated so much, in fact, that Rebel enormously enjoyed the fact that he missed the bottom step of the ladder on his first descent and sat down rather hard in an empty ornament box.

"Try again, hero," she invited with a giggle.

"Unkind," he groaned. "Help me out of this damn—"

"I'm busy." She was sitting cross-legged on the carpet, sorting ornaments into small, neat piles. "Tosh, help him."

It was several minutes before Donovan managed to get Tosh off his lap and himself out of the box. "Was that nice?" he demanded after putting Tosh bodily on the couch and out of his way.

"Was it nice to make fun of me when I got dizzy?"

Donovan sighed. "Touché. Hand me that next string of lights, will you?"

Rebel did as he asked, then frowningly regarded the ornaments piled all around her as he went back up the ladder. "How many kids does Lennox have?" she called up to Donovan.

"Since we're living in his house," Donovan called back, "maybe we'd better call him by his first name."

"I don't remember his first name."

"It's Astaire."

In a bemused voice, Rebel murmured, "Astaire. How could I forget a name like that?" Then, in a stronger voice, he said, "All right then—how many kids does Astaire have?"

"Several." Donovan was making his way back down

the ladder, this time negotiating the hazard carefully. "But only the one son. Why?"

Rebel fretfully rubbed her forehead. "Well, it's these decorations. There are at least a dozen with 'Baby's First Year' on them, some of them recent. And a bunch that were obviously made by kids. Everything from plastic to crystal. It looks like a family—and a big family, at that—collected these things over the years."

"So what's wrong with that?" Donovan asked, making his way back up the ladder. "I imagine that Astaire, like many men of his age, has grandchildren."

"I guess." Rebel frowned again. "But it seems out of character. The man you've told me about just wouldn't have these things lying around for years on end. And why here? Does the family meet here every year for Christmas? Because if so, we'd better make tracks."

"It's more than a week until Christmas; we have plenty of time to close the deal and be out of here before then."

Rebel silently conceded the point but stubbornly went back to her original observation. "I still say it's out of character for him to keep these decorations."

"Why?" Donovan asked reasonably. "Even a rake can have a soft spot for his own flesh and blood, can't he?"

Defeated but still disturbed for some reason, Rebel gestured helplessly. "Okay, okay. I'm outgunned; I can see that. I hate thoroughly rational people."

"Would you love me if I were irrational?" Donovan asked anxiously from halfway up the ladder.

With an effort, Rebel ignored the question. "Are you going to be finished with that any time soon? I've found the angel for the top, and I want to see how it looks."

"The angel comes last," he informed her, apparently undisturbed that she hadn't answered his question.

"Well, hurry up, then. I hope you realize this is going to take all day."

"You have someplace else to go?"

"No, but it's the principle of the thing."

"Always in a hurry. You're going to have to learn to slow down, boss, or you'll have an ulcer before you're thirty."

"I started developing an ulcer the day we met."

"Ouch." Donovan set aside the ladder and began stringing the last group of lights. "Well, at least I've had *some* effect on you."

"Stop fishing."

"My father used to say that one should either fish or cut bait."

"So?"

"So I think I'll keep fishing. Never know what I might catch."

"You might catch something you can't handle," she warned lightly.

"I'll take my chances. Shall I hang the decorations on the top, or will you brave the ladder?"

Rebel blinked at the abrupt change of subject. "You get the top."

"Okay. Stand back."

Rebel found herself relegated to one of the archways while he moved boxes and repositioned the ladder. That done to his satisfaction, he calmly walked over to her, took her in his arms, and kissed her with deliberate thoroughness.

Emerging from the embrace to find her fingers clutching his sweater and her heart pounding, Rebel stared up at him dazedly. "Um...what...?" was all she managed.

Donovan gestured upward with one thumb. "It was too good an opportunity to pass up," he said gravely.

Rebel tipped her head back to stare at the sprig of mistletoe hung neatly in the archway above them. "When did that get there?" she asked blankly.

He managed to leer with his eyebrows. "When you

weren't looking, boss." He patted her on the bottom and headed back for the tree.

Rebel wanted to get mad. Donovan was taking shameless advantage of this entire situation, and she had a perfect right to be furious. The problem was, she didn't feel mad. In fact, she felt like laughing.

Choking back the urge and sighing inwardly at her own inexplicable emotions, Rebel went to help with the tree.

Donovan was frowning down at the decorations on the carpet. "You didn't happen to find a key among this stuff, did you?" he asked hopefully as Rebel joined him.

"What kind of key?" she asked innocently.

"A key suitable for unlocking stubborn chastity belts, as if you didn't know."

"Sorry. Nary a one."

"Damn. I'd hoped I might get lucky."

"I told you—knights don't get custody of keys."

"Then how can I become the lord of the castle?"

"With great difficulty. Here,"—she dumped a handful of ornaments into his outstretched palms—"hang these."

"Will that get me a castle?"

"It'll get you a gold star. Castles come later."

"Oh, really? How much later?"

Rebel gave him a push toward the tree. "If you don't get busy, we'll have this tree decorated just in time for *next* Christmas."

With a gusty sigh, Donovan began climbing the ladder again. "Since you won't answer that question, how about another one?"

"You can ask, but I don't promise to answer." Rebel got busy hanging ornaments on the lower third of the tree.

"Well, I'm curious. When the lord of the castle gets the key, exactly what rights does that give him?"

"Oh, the works." Rebel filled a small box with ornaments and handed it up to him the moment his hands were empty again.

"Define that, please," he requested politely.

"The works? Well, actually, it's more of a partnership deal. The lord and his lady share joint ownership of the castle and everything therein. Tasks are divided according to who does what best. And of course the lady is responsible for the castle whenever his lordship is out jousting or defending the realm from invading hordes, or things like that."

Donovan was shaking with silent laughter. "I'd love to hear you give a talk on medieval history," he murmured.

"Who's talking medieval?" Rebel muttered, but only to herself. Aloud, she said, "Will you please start working your way down? We've got a bare spot in the middle, and I can't reach that high."

"You're rushing again."

"Sorry."

"Forget it. Can I buy a key, by the way?"

"Absolutely not. It has to be given freely."

"Oh. Coercion is out then?"

"Definitely."

"How about blackmail?"

"Unchivalrous."

"What's a knight to do?"

"All things come to he who waits."

"Is that a promise?"

"It's a proverb."

Donovan dropped a cardboard reindeer on her head— deliberately. And then gave her an innocent "Who, me?" look when she glared up at him.

"That wasn't smart, hero. One push from me and we'll be scraping you off the hearth for a week."

"Sorry. It slipped."

"I'll bet."

"Okay, so it didn't slip. But you shouldn't have dashed my hopes like that."

"It hasn't bothered you so far."

"Good thing I thrive on rejection," Donovan responded philosophically.

For once Rebel didn't have a snappy comeback.

The tree was given its finishing touches after dinner that night, and a toast was gravely drunk to usher in the holidays in style. The remainder of the evening was quiet and companionable as they listened to music and watched the lights blinking cheerfully on their gaily decorated tree.

Rebel excused herself fairly early and headed for her room, feeling Donovan's eyes following her and torn between relief and disappointment when he made no move to stop her.

She took a long shower and then climbed into bed with a book she didn't really want to read. When she discovered herself reading the first page for the sixth time, she turned out her lamp and tried to go to sleep.

But sleep eluded her. She tossed and turned, checking the watch on her nightstand at fifteen-minute intervals. The earlier conversations with Donovan, bantering but with an undertone of seriousness, kept playing like a recording in her mind. The kiss beneath the archway flitted through her thoughts.

A muffled thump from the sitting room temporarily interrupted her thoughts. She frowned, listening in the darkness for a few moments, then dismissed the sound. She pounded her pillow energetically and tried to sleep once more.

Finally, Rebel threw back the covers and slipped from the bed. In darkness, she crossed the room to the sitting room door, easing it open. Maybe a change of location would help.

But she didn't leave her bedroom.

Very still, she gazed into the sitting room for a long moment and then soundlessly closed her door again. She leaned against the door, thinking about what she had seen.

Donovan. He'd been standing with his back to her, humming softly to himself and hanging decorations on a lovely, six-foot tree in the corner by the window.

The tree had not been cut like the others, but dug up and potted. And a small, abandoned bird's nest nestled among the needles. While she had watched, Donovan had carefully placed a crystal dove in the nest.

She went back to bed and crawled between the sheets, wondering how he had come to pick that tree. She was certain he hadn't seen her looking at it. Then she dismissed the question. It didn't seem to matter somehow. She knew that she was smiling in the darkness, and she knew somehow that she wouldn't have any more trouble sleeping.

And she didn't.

This time, her dreams were different. This time, no golden key dangled enticingly from a turret. But the drawbridge was lowered to welcome the knight riding triumphantly home . . .

Chapter 6

REBEL WOKE MUCH earlier than usual the next morning, her sense of expectancy puzzling her for a moment. But then she remembered.

Quickly, she rose and began dressing, anxious to go into the sitting room and see the completed tree. She donned an attractive slacks-and-sweater set in an ice-blue color, then pulled on a pair of thick, warm socks. She debated the matter of shoes briefly, but chose not to wear any. She and Donovan seemed to spend most of their time running around in their stocking feet anyway.

Rebel glanced over at the boots placed neatly in one corner and grinned faintly. No matter where she left her shoes, they always reappeared in her room. Their host certainly possessed a well-trained staff!

She brushed her hair thoughtfully, gazing at her reflection in the mirror above the dresser. She looked . . . different. Her eyes were bright and sparkling, the weary look she had noticed at the office gone now. There was a glow to her face, the pallor a thing of the past.

A little wryly but not regretfully she realized that the caricature businesswoman had slipped quietly away. And along with her had gone a few other things as well. The strictly ordered business mind had opened up to allow for feminine thoughts; the company no longer seemed the most important thing in her life; the tension, the guardedness, of years had relaxed.

She felt like a woman again.

Rebel placed the brush on the dresser, seeing in her reflection the smile she had felt last night and feeling strangely lighthearted.

Donovan, she realized, had said little about her "letting her hair down"—literally as well as figuratively—since she'd worn it loose yesterday. And she had a sneaking suspicion that that was because he knew her better than she had ever realized. If he had pounced on the change in her, Rebel would probably have reverted to habit out of sheer perversity. And she was suddenly filled with the amused certainty that he had known that.

There was something, she decided, both unsettling and strangely satisfying about being known that well.

Deliberately leaving her hair hanging straight and shining down her back, Rebel left her room and went into the sitting room. Donovan's bedroom door was closed, and she softly crossed the polished floor to the tree.

It was decorated with shining simplicity, the ornaments all glass and crystal. Rebel wondered how he had managed to find all of them. There were stars, tiny glass reindeers, and turtledoves. Elves winked at her out of crystal eyes, and snowflakes glistened pure white among green needles. And at the top of the tree was not the traditional star or angel, but a miniature castle made of glass, perfect in detail down to the lowered drawbridge.

"Like it?"

The soft question made Rebel turn slowly, and she stared at Donovan as he leaned casually in the doorway to his bedroom. He was dressed, like her, in slacks and a sweater—his a deep blue—and was gazing at her with warm eyes.

"I love it...it's beautiful," she answered huskily. "How did you know I wanted this tree?"

"I just knew."

Rebel shook her head slightly with another glance at the tree. "The ornaments?"

"Questions, questions," he chided gently, walking toward her with his sure-footed grace. "I wanted to do it, and you like it, so that's all that matters."

"Why did you want to do it?" she whispered.

His big hands came to rest on her shoulders, and he smiled down at her with those warm, caressing eyes. "Because I love you."

In that moment, Rebel could have believed him. But it was too perfect, too easy, and the little gremlin in her head wouldn't let her believe. Donovan must have seen the doubt in her eyes, because he immediately drew her into his arms.

"I can't blame you for not trusting," he said with a sigh, resting his chin on top of her head. "Not after what you've been through. Give it time, Rebel. I've been patient this long; I'm not about to pressure you now."

But Rebel could sense the hurt in him, and it disturbed her deeply. She didn't want to hurt him. Even less, though, did she want to expose herself to the kind of hurt another ambitious man could bring.

With his uncanny understanding of her, Donovan seemed to sense that she just wasn't ready to talk seriously. Keeping one arm around her, he began leading her toward the door. "Ready for breakfast, boss?" he asked lightly. "I believe that waffles are on the menu for this morning."

Friday and Saturday followed the easy, playful course they had set for themselves, but tension inevitably grew. Rebel could feel the awareness between them as powerful as a current beneath a thin layer of ice, and it became harder and harder to ignore.

And for that, Donovan was largely responsible. Although the bantering continued, he was clearly determined to show her how much he wanted her. And he found ingenious ways to do that—ways she could find no defense against.

Except, perhaps, for laughter.

It all started with the mistletoe. Donovan had apparently found an enormous cache of the stuff somewhere and had spread it all through the lodge. Every time Rebel turned around, she found herself beneath a sprig of it.

"Donovan!"

"Well, I couldn't ignore the mistletoe."

"Look, Carson saw, and you've offended his dignity."

"Not at all. He's just making himself scarce like the tactful soul he is."

"That mistletoe wasn't there a minute ago!"

"It is now."

"What'd you do—hire a squad of elves?"

"Damn, you guessed it!"

Rebel was attacked beneath mistletoe even where it was nearly impossible for mistletoe to be.

"How much did you pay the stable hand to hang out that window, Donovan?"

"He volunteered. Out of the goodness of his heart."

"You're making a spectacle of me."

"Not at all. All the world loves a lover."

"You're impossible."

"Nothing is impossible. Only improbable."

"All right then—you're improbable."

"Thank you. I'd hate to be dull."

Apparently possessing a singular talent for garnering goodwill—or maybe it was because of the holiday season—Donovan somehow managed to draft the housekeeper, the maids, and Carson as allies. More than once Rebel found mistletoe dangled over her head by a helpful hand—and it wasn't Donovan's.

"How much did you pay her?"

"Nothing. She likes standing on chairs."

"You can get down now, Mrs. Evans. Donovan, you're absolutely, certifiably insane!"

"Sneaky, too."

"Unfair as well. How am I supposed to think when you keep grabbing me?"

"Who's grabbing? I'm just indulging in a holiday tradition."

While the mistletoe was serving its purpose, the entire staff got into the act. Donovan was bent on wooing, and everyone at the lodge was apparently just as bent on helping him.

Candlelight and soft, romantic music graced meals—even breakfast. Books of love poetry began appearing wherever Rebel chose to sit down. Red paper hearts began adorning the various Christmas trees. Even Tosh sported a red ribbon around his neck, from which dangled a paper heart.

"Where did he get that?"

"The elves must have given it to him."

"A six-and-a-half-foot elf, maybe?"

"Christmas makes anything possible."

Wavering beneath the bombardment, torn between laughter and tears half the time, Rebel nonetheless found the strength of mind to bawl out Donovan.

"All right! Breakfast in bed was the last straw! Do you know how embarrassing it was to have Carson and two maids setting a gargantuan feast in my lap?"

"I helped you eat it."

"That's not the point! It was embarrassing!"

"You looked lovely."

"I looked half asleep, dammit. Why don't you just take the easy way out and get me drunk?"

"Would it work?"

"Forget that I said that. You're driving me crazy!"

"Have a glass of wine, boss."

"Donovan, I am going to kill you. Do you hear me? If possible, with my bare hands!"

"That sounds like fun. The bare hands part, I mean."

"What will Astaire think?"

"I'll handle him."

"Why doesn't that comfort me?"

"I don't know."

"And another thing," Rebel began wrathfully, loath to admit herself outgunned yet another time, "I want to know—"

"I can't tell you my little plan to get Astaire here yet."

"*Stop* answering my questions before I ask them!" she wailed, feeling definitely put-upon. "You've been doing it all day! Do you know how unnerving that is?"

"We're attuned," he murmured, a tremor of laughter in his voice.

"I don't care if we're a song!" she snapped, in no mood to search for a better pun. She dropped her head into her hands, muttering to herself. "Why did I come here? Everything's been crazy since I came here. The whole world's gone nuts..." Her head lifted, and she glared at Donovan. "Would you at *least*," she snapped, "have the decency to stop grinning? It's very difficult to yell at a man who won't yell back!"

Standing before the fireplace with his arms folded

across his massive chest, Donovan made no attempt to squelch his lopsided grin. "Two flints make a fire; you'll strike no spark off me, boss," he told her cheerfully.

Rebel lowered her head again, uttering a sound midway between a groan of despair and an ill-suppressed giggle. "You're fired. Go away."

"Who's going to bargain for that land?" he asked practically.

Sitting back on the couch, Rebel carefully crossed one jean-clad leg over the other and stared at him. Truth to tell, she had completely forgotten about the land, and she hoped to heaven that her face didn't give that away. "You're rehired. Temporarily. When's our host returning?"

"Monday afternoon," Donovan answered promptly.

"How did you manage that?"

"Chicanery."

Rebel blinked and fought to hide a smile. "And I'm not to ask exactly what you mean by that?"

"I'd appreciate it."

"What assurance do I have that you're not doing something I wouldn't approve of?"

"None at all. You wouldn't approve."

"Donovan, am I going to have to fire you by the time this is over with?"

"You already have."

"I rehired you. Will I have to fire you again?"

He appeared to give the question serious consideration. "You'll probably want to kill me," he answered at last, his voice oddly whimsical. "Slowly. With your bare hands."

Rebel sat up with a jerk, staring at him in dawning horror. "Donovan . . . what have you done?"

"Would you believe . . . had Astaire Lennox kidnapped?"

It took Rebel only a moment to realize that her leg

was being pulled—by an expert. She sat back with a sigh, the stiffness draining away. "Don't do that to me, dammit. I thought you were serious. What did you really do?"

"Nothing illegal."

Rebel gave up. He wasn't going to tell her. It didn't really bother her, because in business matters she trusted him completely. It was this sudden interest in *her* that she mistrusted.

Donovan came over to sit down beside her on the couch, lifting one of her hands and rubbing it against his cheek. "I wish you wouldn't let it worry you," he said soberly.

Her senses spinning at the loverlike gesture, Rebel said the first thing she could think of. "What—how you're getting Astaire here?"

"No." He sighed roughly, the cheerful teasing gone. "Me. And whether it's you or the company I want."

Rebel made a useless attempt to pull her hand away, still not ready to talk seriously. Still not ready to take *him* seriously. But this time, Donovan wouldn't be denied.

"Rebel, I look at business the way your father does." His voice was quiet, but it held an undertone of urgency. "It's great to build something with your mind and your wits, to watch it grow until it's established. But it's the challenge of the thing that counts, not the end result. I'd be just as happy training horses, or laying bricks, or watching my kids grow up.

"I'm not interested in power. Hell, you said it yourself—I could be my own boss. And I wouldn't need to step on you to do it. I could have started my own company ten years ago; I had the chance. But I passed it up, Rebel. I didn't want or need the headaches, the ulcers, or the backstabbing and the power plays."

Rebel looked at him steadily, trying to understand,

trying to believe. "Then why do you work for me?" she asked finally. "You still end up with twelve-hour days, hurried lunches, board meetings lasting until midnight. No time for a personal life. No time to relax. Just stress and tension and potential ulcers."

"I work for *you*," he agreed, stressing the last word softly. "I took the job a year ago because I knew I'd be working for you; Marc made no secret of the fact that he was ready to retire and that you would take over for him. I wanted to lighten the load for you, Rebel. The company could have gone to hell in a bucket for all I cared—and for all Marc cared, although you don't realize that. But you were totally wrapped up in the business, buried in it, and because of that, I wanted to help you."

"Nobility," she managed with feigned lightness, wondering if what he'd said about her father was true.

"No—enchantment. You were trying to give everything you had to the company—everything your bastard of a husband left you with. It was draining you. I tried to lighten the load for you, but there was only so much you'd let me do."

A faint thread of humor brightened his voice suddenly. "You don't realize the conspiracies your...dedication ...caused. The entire staff did everything possible to help you. A great many minor problems never reached your desk or mine. Business was discussed over lunch or dinner whenever possible, because we'd want to make sure you ate something that day. Bessie deliberately turned off your alarm clock many mornings, just so you'd sleep an extra hour or so. Marc was after me constantly to try to get you to slow down, to convince you that the company wasn't the be-all and end-all of everything. Not that I could. You didn't even see me."

Rebel winced at that last oddly bleak comment. She knew, somehow, that what he said about his efforts, the staff's, Bessie's, was true. With the veils of abstraction stripped away now, she could look back and see much more clearly. And what she saw was, as Donovan had said, a conspiracy—with her in the center of it.

Scolding Bessie because she hadn't awakened her. Donovan's smooth "Don't worry, I handled everything" when she's rushed to the office an hour later. Her executive staff seemingly running itself. Problems solved by the time they filtered through to her. Meetings finished in record time. Bessie mothering her, pestering her to rest, to eat. Donovan making lunch or dinner reservations as a matter of course, arranging discussions across a food-laden table whenever possible.

Donovan... Always the needed bit of information, the shrewd suggestion, the sound advice. Always there when she needed him. Lifting as much of the burden as she allowed—scheming to lift even more. Final decisions always hers, but with his thoughts on them flowing through her mind.

She looked at him blankly, stunned by the fact that she had never seen, never realized. "But, why?" she whispered. "Why did you—all of you—go to all that trouble?"

He pressed a gentle kiss into the palm of her hand. *"We* never doubted you, love," he told her quietly. "From Marc down to the typing pool, none of us doubted that you could run the company—and run it well. But you doubted yourself. You gave the company more than it needed, and it was draining the life out of you. We could all see that. A blind man could have seen it. And none of us wanted to see the company break you."

"This trip...?" Rebel stared at him.

Donovan shrugged slightly, and a glint of mischief showed itself briefly in his eyes. "I could have handled this on my own," he admitted. "But you were strained to the breaking point, and I couldn't stand it any longer.

I had to get you away from the office, if only for a few days."

He looked down at the hand he still held firmly, and then he met her eyes again, his own somber. "Honey, I don't want your company. I wish to hell you didn't want it, either, but I know you do. And I respect that. You're a natural businesswoman; you're shrewd and you're strong and you're capable. Anything less than the full use of your abilities would be sheer waste.

"But there are other things beside business, Rebel. Challenges to stretch your mind the way business does. I think you're beginning to see that now. Or at least considering the possibilities. I hope so. If you ever decide that the business has served its purpose—that you don't want to be chained to a company—I hope you'll let me be there beside you, exploring the possibilities of another kind of life.

"And if not—if the business wins in the end—then I'll still be there. I'll share that with you. Shoulder as much of the load as you'll let me. Bully you, if I have to. I won't let the company have all of you, Rebel."

She tried to shake off the spell of his quiet, almost hypnotic voice. "You—you make the company sound like a rival," she said with an uncertain little laugh.

His smile was twisted, a curious bitterness flashing briefly in his eyes. "Ironic, isn't it?" he said roughly. "You suspect me of wanting the company and intending to use you to get it. And a hundred—a thousand! — times during the past year, I've silently consigned Sinclair Hotels to the fiery depths of hell. If I could bargain with the devil to free you from that company, I'd do it. No matter what the price—except for your unhappiness. I won't bargain with that."

Rebel tried to let his words—and the incredible commitment he had made a year before—sink in and be recognized for the truth she sensed it was. But the little gremlin sneered at her.

Another man had said wonderful, moving things to her. Another man had made lies sound like truth. Another man had acted a part for three years, had possessed her body and her mind and her heart, leaving her shattered and betrayed when the deceit was revealed.

It was too much to think about, too much to unravel. She didn't know whom to trust, what to believe. She knew only that she wouldn't—couldn't—be hurt that way again.

Rebel rose to her feet, gently pulling her hand from Donovan's grasp. "It's late. I think I'll go to bed. Maybe read for a while." She wondered at her own calm, detached voice, the meaningless words. What was wrong with her? Why couldn't she respond to the pain in his eyes, the look of defeat on his face?

"Good night, Rebel." His voice was toneless.

She turned away from him and walked steadily through the archway and into their wing. Something was pulling at her, ordering her, screaming at her to go back to him. Something was telling her that she was walking away from something infinitely precious.

Steadily, she walked on.

In her own room, she showered, changed into a fresh, flower-sprigged satin nightgown, and brushed her hair. Then she paced. Back and forth, from window to door, steadily, constantly.

Images flashed through her mind. Bantering conversations. A mythical key. A Christmas tree decorated with laughter. One decorated in secret, as a gift. Kisses beneath mistletoe. The dammed-up tears of too many years, shed at last. Strong arms holding her, a gentle order to blow her nose. Questions answered before they were asked. Burdens lifted, burdens shared. Light comments taken seriously. Serious comments taken lightly. A smile in the darkness, and dreams of castles and knights.

Rebel heard Donovan go into his bedroom; still she paced. There was something teasing her, something battering for admittance into her mind. But pain-filled violet eyes kept haunting her. She had never intentionally hurt another human being before. But tonight she had hurt Donovan.

Defeated. Donovan defeated. She couldn't bear to see that, couldn't bear to see the chinks in his armor. It hurt her. In hurting him, she had hurt herself. That meant something. That had to mean something. But what?

Gradually the fragments and questions faded into blankness. Her pacing slowed, finally stopped. She felt, oddly, that she had been walking in her sleep. Quietly, she opened her bedroom door and went out into the sitting room. A fire had been freshly built in the hearth, as it was every night.

Unable to resist the thick fur rug in front of the fireplace, Rebel sank down into its white softness. The room was lit only by firelight, the silence disturbed by pops and crackles and an occasional soft moan as the wind picked up outside.

Rebel rolled over onto her stomach, propped up on her elbows as she stared into the fire. The gremlin was silent. There were no more arguments to voice. Donovan's strength she could fight with her own, but his defeat left her defenseless. She couldn't think anymore; she could only feel. And what she felt was the desire, the need that had been building for days.

This room demanded a lover, she realized dreamily, and she made no attempt to banish the thought. A lover, coming out of the surrounding darkness and into firelight, silent and strong and as raw as nature had made him. A man filled with tenderness and sensitivity and aching need.

Eyes slitted against the fire's shifting orange glow,

she allowed her mind to sketch the lover. Big. A big man with broad shoulders and a massive chest, long, powerful arms and legs. Moving like a jungle cat. Black hair a little shaggy, going silver at the temples. A face that might have been hard but wasn't. An elusive dimple in one lean cheek. Striking, startling, incredibly vivid violet eyes.

Donovan. She needed him. She needed his warmth and his closeness. Needed to try to heal the hurt she had inflicted. Needed him to begin to heal the hurt inside herself. She needed to make a commitment she could not yet make in words.

The thoughts had barely peaked in her consciousness when a small sound drew her eyes. And there the lover stood. Her lover.

Firelight glinted off his body, naked but for the towel knotted around his lean waist. Even as she watched, the towel fell. Huge, silent, he was overwhelmingly male and devastatingly handsome. And the aching need she had dreamed of was evident in every taut, hard line of his body.

And in his eyes was the look of a man reprieved from hell.

Rebel turned off her conscious mind at that point. He had come to her, and nothing else mattered. For this night, at least, he would belong to her. Her man.

Donovan moved toward her slowly, as if he were approaching a deer he was wary of frightening. Muscles rippled smoothly beneath his shimmering flesh, drawing her fascinated eyes. She remained on her stomach as he knelt beside her on the fur rug. Even as she looked away from him she could feel his presence through her every pore and nerve ending. And her body tensed like a drawn bow when she felt his big hand come out to rest lightly on the small of her back.

Still, she didn't turn her head, waiting breathlessly

for the next touch. It came. His free hand brushed aside her long hair, and she felt his warm lips moving over the sensitive nape of her neck. Rebel bowed her head slightly, one kind of tension melting away and a new kind taking its place. The hand on her back was moving gently, a finger languidly tracing her spine through the sheer satin of her gown. His other hand had brushed away the lacy straps, fingers exploring the delicate bones of her shoulders with the seeking touch of a blind man.

Neither of them uttered a word or made a sound.

She could feel his powerful thigh against her side, the darting touch of his tongue on her flesh, and a shiver began somewhere deep inside her, radiating outward in ripples of sensation. His hand slid down over her hip, her thigh, using the silky material of her gown to create a sensual friction.

Unhurriedly, gently, as though they had all the time in the world, Donovan guided her with soft pressure until she was lying flat on her stomach, arms at her sides and face turned toward him. Her eyes were nearly closed, her breath coming shallowly from between barely parted lips. She was completely quiescent, allowing him to do what he would.

The gown was slowly pulled down, a strong hand beneath her stomach lifting slightly until the material was past her hips and gone. She felt cool air on her skin, heard a soft, rough intake of breath from him, and still didn't look directly at him, didn't move. Now she felt the length of him beside her, felt the thick mat of hair on his chest brushing her back as his lips returned to her neck.

Large hands moved over her body—her back, her hips, her thighs. Touching, stroking, shaping. His mouth followed, tongue darting out again and again to find shiveringly sensitive areas, teeth nipping lightly. Only when he had explored every inch of her flesh between neck and ankles did he gently turn her over onto her back.

Rebel's lashes drifted up as she looked fully at him for the first time since he'd begun touching her. His oddly fixed stare was gliding down her body slowly, leaving a trail of fire. And then his eyes met hers, and the breath caught in her throat. She had never seen such hunger in a man's eyes, such aching need, and for a moment it frightened her. But only for a moment.

His dark head bent toward hers slowly until their lips were only a breath apart. Teasingly, he kissed her once, twice, kisses no heavier than dew. It was Rebel who finally broke the silence between them, moaning softly as her arm moved at last to encircle his neck. As though the involuntary sound were the signal he'd been waiting for, Donovan abandoned his tormenting, taking her mouth in a surge of ravenous hunger.

And it *was* hunger, the same almost desperate hunger she'd seen in his eyes. Like a man lost and wandering in a bleak desert for a very long time, he came at last to an oasis, drinking from a clear pool and devouring tender fruit. He couldn't seem to get enough, couldn't slake his thirst or satisfy his hunger.

His strange, inexplicable desperation moved Rebel in some way she couldn't name. She could feel his heart pounding out of control in the massive chest pressed against her, could feel the rigid desire throbbing against her thigh. His intense, fervent need transmitted itself to her, and her own need spiraled crazily.

Her fingers locked together with almost bruising strength; tongues met, clashed, possessed, dueled as though to the death—or to life.

The need for oxygen finally proved stronger than anything else—but barely. Donovan drew a single harsh breath when his lips reluctantly left hers. She was granted only a glimpse of his taut expression, a flash of violet eyes darkened to purple, and then his face was buried between her breasts.

Rebel pulled air into her starved lungs in shaken gasps, her fingers still tangled in his hair. Large hands slid up her body to shape full breasts; lips moved from one hardened tip to the other. He lavished her breasts with adoring kisses, his tongue curling voraciously around the hard bud his mouth held. Sensually abrasive hands spanned her waist, traced the curve of her hips, feathered along the inside of her thighs.

Jerking involuntarily, Rebel moaned when his searching fingers found the warm, wet center of her desire. Her body arched of its own accord, her fingers sliding from his hair to dig into the muscles of his back. His probing touch was sending her senses on a crazy, cartwheeling spin, and she couldn't find the breath to tell him what he was doing to her.

Oh, God, he was so gentle! In spite of the desperate need she could feel burning in him, in spite of the almost inhuman control that made his muscles bunched and rigid beneath her fingers, he was so very gentle. And she couldn't even tell him what that meant to her.

He raised his head at last, and Rebel tugged mutely at his shoulder, unable to even whisper a plea. But he knew; he understood. Her legs shifted restlessly as he slid between them, and she suddenly knew a fierce need to feel his heavy body bearing down on her, crushing her into the pile of the rug beneath them.

But he hesitated, staring down at her, breathing like a marathon runner at the end of a very long race. She saw something flicker in his desire-darkened eyes, something uncertain, oddly defensive, and understanding came clearly to her mind. He was afraid he'd hurt her!

Her arms encircled his neck, pulling his head down until she could reach his mouth, telling him in the best way she knew that he wouldn't hurt her.

Donovan's groan rumbled from deep in his chest, accepting her silent assurance as his wonderful weight bore her down into the rug. Rebel's breath somehow got lost, leaving her body as he entered it. She felt like a virgin again, knowing a man for the first time, being known in a way one could never describe but only feel. And it had never felt this way before.

He was with her, filling the hollowness that had ached for him, filling her until she was conscious only of him. He was still for a moment, as though possessing her satisfied something in him that was beyond words, beyond description. And then he was moving gracefully, powerfully, but with great tenderness, his eyes blazing darkly out of his taut face.

Rebel held him, moved with him, feeling the primitive, driving tension building within her until she felt that she would shatter into a million pieces. And for one eternal second, she thought that she had done just that. She was flying apart, jagged pieces of herself soaring with exquisite agony. She was unable to cry out; only a strangled, kittenlike sound escaped her. She was aware dimly of a shuddering groan torn from Donovan's throat.

Donovan's heavy weight continued to crush her body into the rug, but Rebel felt only contentment. As though they were the epicenter of some massive earthquake, she could feel aftershocks, shudders in his body and her own. His face was buried in the curve of her neck; his harsh breathing gradually steadied in her ear.

He rolled slowly onto his side, taking her with him, his lips seeking hers almost blindly. Powerful arms held her securely to him, bodies touching, merging. He kissed her hungrily, as if only the sharp edge of his need had been blunted.

He had left a tiny glowing ember deep inside of her, and expertly he fanned it to flame again.

Rebel was aware of very little clear, conscious thought

during the hours that followed. But her occasional, stray thoughts were delighted ones. She had never known, never believed, that lovemaking could be this way. He silently taught her things about herself, her body, that she had never known before, and Rebel learned each lesson blissfully.

With the openness of old lovers, the silent, instinctive understanding of soul mates, they explored each other long into the night. The need continued to drive them both, each touch and kiss sensitizing their flesh until the brush of fingers and lips—even the meeting of eyes— was like a torch branding raw nerves. It was almost unbearable, and yet it was borne; almost agony, and yet it was sweet...so sweet.

Again and again they made the journey of lovers, leaving earthly ties far behind them and passing an oc- casional shooting star along the way, then drifting slowly down, only to begin the dizzying climb again.

Dawn's light was beginning to creep into the room, the fire in the hearth long since ashes, when Rebel finally yielded to exhaustion. His hands were caressing again with a touch she recognized, the hunger in him apparently insatiable, but she was just too tired to respond. With an apologetic murmur, she buried her face in the damp curve of his neck, utterly limp and delightfully weary.

Immediately his touch changed, becoming gentle and soothing. He stroked her back, her hair. She felt his heart beating steadily against her, the warmth of his body off- setting the chill of the room. The imprint of his large body, the touch of his hands, the throb of his heart, all followed her into dream.

Chapter 7

WHEN REBEL AWOKE, she didn't open her eyes for a long moment. Somehow, she was aware of being watched, and she knew instantly who was watching her. Donovan. She could feel his warmth beside her in bed, hear his steady breathing. When had he carried her to bed? She didn't remember. But she remembered everything else.

Physically, she'd never felt better. Emotionally, she was teetering on the edge of a precipice, clinging to finger- and toeholds. One sudden or wrong move, and over she'd go.

Rebel didn't bother to belatedly acknowledge—even to herself—that she was in love with Donovan. She'd known that for quite some time now. What she did silently acknowledge was the fact that she was still confused. She needed time.

"Are you going to feign sleep all day?"

The deep, amused voice brought Rebel's eyes open with a snap. She was lying on her back, close beside Donovan. He was raised up on one elbow, watching her with mock gravity.

"Good morning," she murmured. "Or is it?"

"Actually, it's after noon," he told her.

"Oh." For the life of her, Rebel couldn't think of a thing to say. She was highly conscious of the hard length of his body beside hers, and she wondered what on earth she should talk about with the man who had ravished her delightfully for the better part of a night.

"You're blushing!" he said in a delighted voice, beginning to chuckle softly.

"I am not." She forced every ounce of dignity possible into the three small words. "You're seeing things."

"No, you're definitely blushing."

"Stop harping."

"Yes, ma'am." He leaned over to kiss her, his lips warm and lazy. Last night's desperation was gone, but his hunger had not diminished a bit.

Rebel found her arms creeping up around his neck, her mouth responding to his, and decided that conversation wasn't all that important anyway. She felt his arms drawing her close. In the back of her mind the gremlin remained silent.

Donovan raised his head slightly, gazing down at her with smoky purple eyes. "Tell me something, lady of the castle," he murmured. "Is the key mine, or am I just . . . borrowing it?"

Rebel didn't lower her arms, her fingers still tangled in his shaggy black hair. His steady eyes demanded honesty, and she gave it, quietly, her voice a little husky. "I need time, Donovan. Time to . . . get my priorities in order."

He was silent for a moment, and then he nodded. In

a voice of utter calm, he told her, "Take all the time you need, honey. But I'd better warn you about something. The only way you'll keep me out of your bed from now on is with a loaded gun."

Rebel blinked at him. "Masterful, aren't you?" she murmured, chuckling.

"I'd be glad to demonstrate," he muttered, beginning to nuzzle her throat, "exactly how masterful I can be."

She decided that there was something wicked about making love in the middle of the day. Wonderfully wicked.

Whatever constraint had existed between them vanished rapidly. If Donovan was disturbed by her continued reluctance to make a verbal commitment, he gave no sign of it. He was cheerful again, teasing, bantering. The only difference in his manner toward her was an indefinably male look in his eyes whenever they rested on her.

They shared a bath in the huge tub in Rebel's bathroom and then dressed casually and ate a well-prepared brunch in the dining room. Rebel wasn't even surprised to find the meal ready and waiting for them; she'd already come to the private conclusion that Carson was a wizard.

After brunch they went for a walk outside, their boots crunching through the additional two inches of snow that had fallen during the night. Rebel had hoped that the cold air would clear away the remaining cobwebs in her mind, allowing her to think clearly, but she was granted no such luck.

Donovan held her hand firmly, swinging it between them cheerfully like a teenager, warm eyes on her almost constantly. And she couldn't resist that. She felt cared for, cherished, and not even the occasional whisperings of the gremlin could fight that.

Wandering along one of the many trails that spread out from the lodge, she finally worked up the courage to ask about something that had been puzzling her. She wasn't sure she wanted to know the answer, but the question wouldn't leave her alone.

"Donovan . . . this past year . . ."

"What about it, love?"

How easily the endearments rose to his lips, she thought. That had never been easy for her. Never. She shunted aside the thought. "

"I never noticed—I mean, there was never any sign of . . ." Floundering helplessly, she sent an oblique glance up at him, silently begging him to help her out.

"Women?" he supplied, his faintly amused eyes meeting hers before she quickly looked away again. "That's because there weren't any—except for a certain company president."

"None at all? I mean, not even casual. . ." Floundering again, she silently cursed her stumbling tongue.

"Not even casual," he murmured. "I wanted you, Rebel."

A year, she thought faintly. She tried to understand what he must have gone through. And worst of all— worst of all was that she had never known, never *seen*.

This new revelation made his gentleness of the night before even more astonishing. It spoke volumes for his self-control, his restraint. She had felt the desperate need within him, had seen it in his eyes, but never once had he rushed her, never once had he hurt her.

"It wasn't easy," Donovan murmured musingly as both of them came to a stop.

The curving trail provided a natural vantage point here, the ground falling away in a sheer drop beside the path. The entrance to a snow-blanketed valley lay before them, the pristine beauty of the snow untouched by man or machine. Lonely and beautiful.

"There were times," Donovan continued, "when I wanted to just grab you and shake you until you looked at me. Saw me. Hell, I wasn't even sure you'd like what you saw. But I was willing to take that chance. I had to. I never had a choice. So I stuck around and tried to become important to you in any way I could."

"My right hand," she murmured, staring out over the valley but not really seeing it.

"Yeah." He sighed roughly. "It wasn't what I wanted, but it helped you and kept me near you. I spent a lot of nights pacing the floor and wondering if I were...tilting at windmills. Then I'd look at you in the office the next morning and know that I was stuck there. For however long it took."

Rebel gently disengaged her hand from his and moved to the edge of the path. "I'm sorry," she murmured, again staring without seeing the view.

He came up behind her and put his arms around her, drawing her back against him. "Don't be. You couldn't help not seeing me any more than I could help staying."

She stirred slightly but made no attempt to leave the warmth of his embrace. "I still don't know very much about you. You said you were an only child?"

"No, I said that I was an 'only,'" he corrected. "An only son. I have sisters."

"Really? How many?"

"Six—all older than I." He chuckled softly. "Dad said that he wasn't going down without a fight. If I'd been another girl, he was going to throw away his vitamins and try something else."

Rebel found herself smiling. "And your mother?"

"She said that six girls were enough; they already had more than they needed for a basketball team."

Awe in her voice, Rebel asked, "Are they all as tall as you?"

"No, but none of them is small."

"I've always wondered what it would be like to have a large family—no pun intended."

He laughed again. "Marry me and find out," he invited easily. "My family's generally pretty far-flung, but we manage to get together a few times a year. Want to meet them?"

Rebel ignored the suggestion in favor of the question. "Maybe someday," she answered evasively, then immediately changed the subject. "Whom do you resemble—your mother or father?"

"Both," he responded, allowing the subject change. "I have Dad's coloring and Mom's features. And, before you ask, the girls all got Mom's red hair."

"All of them?"

"Various shades, but all red."

"Must be a temperamental family."

Donovan reflected for a moment. "Not really. Helen—she's the next step up in age after me—has a temper like a drunk marine. But she cheerfully lets her kids bully her, and although my brother-in-law says they go through at least one set of china a month, he doesn't seem to mind."

Rebel laughed, then urged, "Keep climbing the steps. This is getting interesting."

"Are you sure you're warm enough?" he asked. "We could continue this inside, if you'd rather."

"I'm warm enough." Rebel tipped back her head to rest against his shoulder. "Keep climbing."

"Whatever the lady wants. Next is Geneva."

"Unusual name," Rebel commented.

"You don't have to tell me that. Gen's complained bitterly about it for as long as I can remember. It means 'juniper tree,' and she's never forgiven Dad for that; it was his inspiration."

Victim herself of an unusual name, Rebel could well imagine how Donovan's sister felt. "I'm surprised she's still speaking to him. What's she like?"

"She . . . *arranges* things," Donovan said carefully.

"Ruthlessly and with every good intention in the world. She imagines boredom in every silence, and inactivity drives her crazy. So she keeps people busy—whether they want to be or not. Her kids claim that any general could use her expertise to straighten out his troop movements. And her husband, Adam, told me that when they spent a few weeks in Hawaii last year, Gen arranged two marriages in a bewildered island family and then topped off her vacation by preventing a volcanic erruption. Singlehandedly."

This time, Rebel hooted with delight. "She sounds daunting."

"Not at all. Adam adores her, and the kids listen respectfully to her advice and then do exactly as they please."

"Brave kids. Next step, please."

"Charley—Charlotte. She's vague, absentminded, and creative. Talks a mile a minute and never makes sense—although she never misses a thing. Her husband, Rick, calls her half-pint because she's the smallest of us all."

"Back up a minute," Rebel requested. "Who's Helen's husband?"

"Burke."

"Okay. I'm trying to keep the names straight. Next step."

"Ami. Her kids are all out of the nest, her husband is Steve, and she's the original 'iron hand in the velvet glove.' She could smile sweetly at opposing sides in a war and have them laying down arms before they'd know what hit them. Steve says he was on his honeymoon before he came out of the daze, and by then he didn't have the energy to protest."

Rebel bit her lip. "Next step," she ordered unsteadily.

"Judith," Donovan said obediently. "And Judith is sunshine. She's happy and cheerful and never sees the bad in people. Her husband, Larry, and her kids say that she could daunt the devil. Everyone she meets is a friend, and nobody ever has to ask her for help with a problem."

"Is my counting off," Rebel murmured, "or are we at the last step now?"

"Last. Or first, depending on which way you're going. Oldest of us all is Kelly. She's . . . queenly. Reminds me of a battleship under full steam." After a moment and a giggle from Rebel, he added fairly, "That could be pure prejudice on my part; eleven years' age difference rendered my childhood hideous with bullying."

"Forgive me if I don't believe that," Rebel murmured wryly.

"Shrewd of you. Actually, she's got a heart like oatmeal, although you'd never guess it. Kelly is loud and astringent and will hotly debate anything at the drop of a hat. Her husband, Robert, trails along in her wake, bemused and soft-spoken. Contrary to appearances, Robert can shut Kelly up with a word or a look; she absolutely adores him."

"Interesting family," Rebel said at last.

"We have an opening. Want to enlist?"

Rebel ignored that. "Are you a great-uncle yet?"

"Well, of course I'm a great uncle."

"You know what I mean."

Donovan chuckled. "Right. Well, Ami, Judith, and Kelly all have kids who married fairly young, so there are several babies and toddlers in the family. I'm definitely a great-uncle."

"Must be a madhouse when you all get together," Rebel said, hearing the note of envy in her own voice.

"Utter bedlam. Mom and Dad are both in their seventies, and Dad swears after every gathering that he'll never make it through another one. But he's usually the first to suggest we all get together for Arbor Day or something. One year he called us all together to celebrate the first rose in his garden."

Rebel smiled. "He sounds terrific."

"He is." There was a wealth of pride and affection in Donovan's voice. "I wish I had half his energy and a quarter of his wisdom. He's the undisputed patriarch of the family, and Mom rules *him* with an iron hand." After a pause, he added, "They remind me a lot of your parents. Totally devoted to one another, but still individuals after years of marriage."

Bemused, Rebel murmured, "I didn't know you'd met my mother. When she and Dad make flying visits to Dallas, she never comes to the office."

"She did in July. You and Marc had flown to Tahoe to check on that hotel and left me to mind the store. I took Vanessa out to lunch and then we went to the zoo."

"You did?" Rebel said blankly.

"Sure we did. Actually, I would have met her sooner, except that while I was working for Marc she was already in Paris decorating the house they'd bought. A charming lady, Vanessa."

Rebel wondered vaguely why she wasn't shocked at Donovan's familiarity with her parents. His next words, however, drove the speculation from her mind.

"We spent the afternoon talking," he added musingly. "She was quite pleased when I told her I was going to marry her daughter."

"You did *what?*" Rebel broke free of his hug and whirled to stare up at him. "You told her—"

"That I was going to marry her daughter." His violet eyes laughed down at her. "One day or another. Fair means or foul. Even if I had to use caveman tactics."

"Donovan, you—you—" Rebel was torn between incredulity and wrath.

"You can hit me if you want," he told her soothingly. "I promise to take it like a man."

Rebel lifted her hand, but it was only to jab a finger into his chest. Each jab emphasized a word. "How dare you tell my mother something like that! What makes you so damn sure—"

Donovan caught her hand and lifted it to his lips. "Honey, one way or another, I'm going to get you the the altar. I don't expect it to be easy, and truth to tell, I wouldn't miss the fight for anything. But I'll win." Disarming her immediately, he added softly, "I have to. Nothing else bears thinking of."

"Don't *say* things like that!" she very nearly wailed, glaring up at him. "You're boxing me in, dammit!"

He grinned and, still holding her hand, began leading her back along the path to the lodge. "I'll give you all the time you need," he offered cheerfully.

"Oh, sure," she muttered. "I can just *feel* all the time you're giving me. Shall we dance the ''Minute Waltz' while we're waiting?"

"Not in the snow," he responded gravely.

She ignored that. She was getting very good at ignoring most of his cute comments. "Donovan, you're taking entirely too much for granted. This is the twentieth century, remember? Standards have changed. *People* have changed."

"All of which has nothing to do with us."

Rebel tried again. It was difficult to think of sensible things to say and watch her footing in the snow at the same time, but she managed. "What I'm trying to say is that nothing in—our relationship automatically implies marriage. It's not written in stone anymore. No one would be shocked if we decided to live together—"

"I would."

"You'd be shocked?"

"Certainly I would. What kind of man do you think I am?"

Rebel bit back a giggle at his offended tone, and then fiercely tried to hang on to her objections. "Donovan . . ."

"Honey, don't waste your breath," he advised calmly. "I don't like unofficial vows with plenty of escape clauses thrown in, and that's what living together would mean. I want everything official. I want the kind of marriage your parents, my parents, and my sisters have—an enduring marriage filled with love."

Rebel swallowed hard. "You're an idealist," she murmured.

"I am that," he agreed, tucking her hand into the crook of his arm as they neared the lodge. "But I'm also blessed with a streak of practicality a yard wide—from my Scottish ancestors, no doubt. And I'm old enough to know what I want, Rebel. You and I will have many a disagreement, I'm sure. You're Irish-German and I'm Scottish-English—with an Indian or two a few generations back—and if anything, that's a combustible mixture. But we'll make it work for us. I have a lot of faith in what we have together."

In the face of that kind of determination, there wasn't much Rebel could say. Although it was true that a part of her was warmed by that determination, she knew what the biggest problem was between them, and she reluctantly brought that up.

"Donovan, even if—even if I'm sure you don't want the company, it's still *there*. And to you, it's a rival."

He stopped on the path and turned to face her, his hand still covering her hand as it rested on his arm. His lean face was serious, his violet eyes grave. "That's true. But understand something, Rebel—I won't ask you to give up the company. If you decide to keep on running it, that's fine. I'll help in every way I can. I won't like it, but I promise not to try to stop you.

"On the other hand, I think we'd both be happier out of the rat race. There are all kinds of possibilities to explore. Sinclair Hotels is an established corporation.

The growth potential is still there, but where's the challenge? What's the point of working the same job day after day? Slight ups and downs due to temperamental co-workers or other people you have to deal with; high-pressure meetings; whirlwind flights around the country. It all gets routine after a while."

Rebel was staring up at him, halted in a seven-year journey by a fork in the road. Which way to go? Slowly, she asked him, "What would you like to do, Donovan? I mean, if it were completely up to you to decide?"

"Besides spend the rest of my life with you?" Donovan gazed off into the distance, thoughtful, considering. "Have a ranch somewhere I think. Raise horses. That's a business, too, of course, but it has enormous benefits. No stuffy offices, for one thing. No high-pressure meetings. No traffic jams to contend with. Just lots of fresh air and sunshine and working with your hands."

His eyes dropped back to hers, and he smiled slowly. "Like I said, I'm not interested in power. I'd much rather . . . plant a fig tree, nurture it, and watch it grow."

"You're an . . . unusual man," she murmured.

"Not really. I think most men would give up the corporate game in a minute if they had a choice. Aside from a relatively rare power-hungry one."

"But you're so good at the corporate game."

He shrugged slightly, his eyes distant again although still fixed on her face. "I suppose, but I'm not really comfortable with it, Rebel. Maybe it's the idealist in me. What's the point of having a success label stuck on me, or money I'll never need? I'd rather enjoy life."

Donovan paused for a moment, and then smiled suddenly. "Remember a while back during that last solar eclipse? There was some guy selling cans of 'solar dark' at a buck a throw. Now that man enjoyed life—and its absurdities."

Rebel felt a smile tugging at her lips. "How many cans did you buy?" she asked, beginning, at last to understand this man.

He grinned. "Just one."

"I bought two," she told him solemnly.

Donovan laughed and began leading her toward the lodge again. "See? We're more alike than you thought."

"I'm beginning to think so. Did you have a pet rock?"

"A niece sent me one for my birthday. How about you?"

"A present from Dad."

"Sounds like Marc. Who gave you the teddy bear?"

Rebel stopped walking abruptly, drawing him to a stop. "How did you know about that?" she asked blankly, thinking to herself that this was the most disjointed walk— and talk—they'd ever had.

Donovan had the grace to look slightly sheepish. "I snooped. One of those work sessions in your apartment. You went to answer the phone or something, and I spent the time looking around. That battered, moth-eaten teddy bear stuck out like a sore thumb in your beautiful Oriental bedroom. It gave me hope."

"It did?"

"Sure. It didn't fit in with your solid businesswoman front. I decided that somewhere underneath all that gray flannel there had to be a woman who could still hang on to a part of childhood."

Rebel thought about that as they started walking again. "You shouldn't have snooped," she said at last, weakly.

"I'm ashamed of myself," he said in a voice that held no sign of shame."

"Sure you are."

"Really."

"Uh-huh."

"And if you believe that," he murmured thoughtfully,

"I have a bridge I'll sell to you. Across the San Francisco Bay. Or there's a big clock in a tower. Or there's the Great Sahara Forest—"

"I get the point. And I'm surprised you weren't selling cans of 'solar dark' yourself."

"Don't be ridiculous. I have the stardust concession."

"Shame on you. Taking advantage of gullible people."

"Nonsense. Want to buy a pinch of stardust? Guaranteed to cure all aches and ills."

"I'm not gullible."

"You bought the dark," he pointed out gravely.

"Don't rub it in. Besides, you bought some, too."

"Ah! But I never claimed not to be gullible."

"There's probably a word for what you *are*, but if there is, I don't know it."

"Charming?"

"I don't think so."

"Lovable?"

"Not quite what I had in mind."

"Irresistible?"

"Hardly."

"Now you've cut me to the quick."

"I'll bet." Rebel sighed. "Never mind. I'll come up with it eventually. I have a feeling it's more along the lines of impossible."

By this time they had crossed between two of the helipads and reached the bottom of the stone steps leading up to the lodge's main entrance. Rebel glanced up at the central A-frame as Donovan laughed, and then she froze, adding yet another temporary halt to their walk.

There was a man standing at the top of the steps. He was tall, lean, hard. He didn't look to be in his late sixties, although Rebel knew he was. He had a full head of copper hair, touched by gray only at the temples. He stood with arms folded, looking down on them from Olympian heights.

"Master of all he surveys," Rebel murmured involuntarily.

"Damn. He's a day early." Donovan did not sound pleased.

Rebel gave him a curious look as they started up the steps, belatedly remembering to remove her hand from his arm. "I thought you had it all arranged for him to come tomorrow."

"I thought the same thing." Donovan glanced down and met her puzzled look. He grimaced slightly. "I was hoping we'd have more time to be alone."

"Before the charades, you mean?"

"Something like that."

An elusive note in Donovan's voice bothered Rebel, and she tried to pin it down. Constraint? Uneasiness? Was he worried about carrying off his role as boss? As soon as the question posed itself, she gave it a mental dismissal. That wasn't it. Then what?

"Mr. Lennox," Donovan called out coolly as they reached the top of the steps and their host, "I'm Donovan Knight. This is my assistant, Rebel Anderson."

As Astaire Lennox held out a hand to Donovan, smiling with some inner amusement, Rebel was experiencing a weird and muddled sense of *déjà vu*.

She had seen this man before somewhere. Not a photo—in the flesh. But she couldn't recall where or when. In the moment or so granted to her for a quick memory check, she studied his face carefully. Lined with age but alive, vital, deeply tanned. His eyes were deep-set, shrewd, and as clear blue as her own. He looked like a tough man, but by no means a stupid one. And although it certainly didn't jibe with Donovan's description of the man, met across a business desk she would have instinctively trusted him. But she couldn't for the life of her recall where she had seen him before, or why he would otherwise seem so familiar.

"Miss Anderson," he said, holding out a hand to her.

"Rebel," she murmured. His grip was firm and friendly without being the slightest bit supercilious. The blue eyes met hers in an amicable, slightly measuring look.

Obeying his almost courtly gesture, she silently preceded the men into the lodge, hearing behind her Lennox cheerfully apologizing to Donovan for the delay in his arrival. Rebel and Donovan removed their coats along with their host, Carson appearing magically out of nowhere to whisk them away. They made their way into the greatroom and sat down.

Rebel listened quietly as the two men talked casually. Her silence was due not to the reticence expected of a secretary but rather to her mental activity.

There was, she decided, something very rotten in the state of Denmark.

She tuned out the conversation. Bits of conversation were briefly reviewed in her mind—light comments, warning comments. Feudal lords with octopus hands. Knight-errantry and an unexpected kiss on the steps.

A method to the madness? Oh, yes. Definitely yes.

"Don't you agree, Rebel?"

She looked up, blinking at the jovial question from Lennox. "I'm sorry?"

"I said that your boss certainly goes after something once he's made up his mind. Wouldn't you agree?"

Rebel turned a limpid gaze to her "boss." In a voice that could have put honeybees out of business, she murmured, "Oh, I certainly agree. He doesn't let anything stand in his way."

Donovan very nearly winced.

"Pass the soap, please."

"Get it yourself."

"Rebel, I've explained why I—uh—exaggerated certain of Astaire's characteristics. I was trying to get through those walls of yours, and I thought that a bit of knight-errantry—"

"You've explained."

Donovan sighed and tried a change of subject. "Did you have to use lilac-scented bubble bath? Astaire will think I'm crazy."

"Just be glad I didn't follow my impulses and pour acid in the tub. You deserved that."

"Rebel . . ."

"You're an impossible man. Pardon me—improbable. Tell me, is it at least true that Astaire doesn't deal with female executives?"

"You read my report."

"Big deal."

"It's true. Just ask him."

"If I didn't want that land—"

"I know, I know. Forgive me?"

"Stop that. You want me to drown?"

"I have marvelous balance."

"You'd have to. And nerves of steel. A sane man wouldn't try that maneuver in a bathtub full of bubbles."

"Look at the fun he'd be missing."

"Donovan, we have to get ready for dinner. Donovan? What're you—? I think that's illegal."

"I must break the law more often."

"Donovan . . . ?"

"Astaire won't mind if we're a little late . . ."

Chapter 8

DURING THE NEXT two days, Rebel found that her role as secretary made her an observer, a listener, and she was surprised to find that very little different from her actions as a boss. It was eerie in a way, she decided—the extremely thin line separating one link of the executive chain from another.

As a boss, she had listened to opinions and recommendations, bits of information needed to make a decision. It had usually been Donovan who had given her the pertinent facts, along with his opinions and advice. She had listened, thought about it, and then decided.

They had worked as a team, each half as important as the other, she realized. Slowly the line in her mind separating employer from employee thinned even more.

Several small things were coming together, pieces assembling a jigsaw puzzle. The first pieces had come together when she had realized on meeting Astaire that Donovan had created a rake where none existed.

Astaire Lennox treated her rather like a daughter. He was friendly, amusing, and unusually down-to-earth for a man of his wealth and power. He made not a single sneering reference to women in corporate positions, women as sexual toys, or anything else that could have been considered sexist.

Those several pieces gradually formed a corner of the puzzle in Rebel's mind. Donovan had been determined to get her up here to this lodge, and he had been perfectly willing to resort to subterfuge to do it.

She could have accepted his reason for that: She was tired and strained, and he'd wanted to get her away from the office. Added to that was his impatience after a year of waiting for her to come out of her chrysalis. Hence the knight-errantry and his immediate moves to take advantage of the situation he had created.

But the puzzle still wasn't complete.

Silently, Rebel watched and listened to the fencing between Donovan and Astaire. It was highly skilled, adroit, and never seemed to accomplish a thing. Rapidly losing interest in the land she needed and increasingly absorbed by the human drama unfolding around her, Rebel made no attempt to berate Donovan for his lack of progress in acquiring the property.

It was slowly dawning on her that Donovan—and perhaps Astaire as well—was deliberately dragging out the negotiations. She didn't know why, but for some reason neither was in any hurry to close the deal. It gave her food for thought.

Rebel wouldn't have been so tolerant of the situation had she not gotten her own priorities into order. She wasn't certain exactly what had finally decided her. The nights with Donovan might had had something to do with it. Making love with him, she had discovered, was a very special kind of sharing. Donovan gave totally of himself, sometimes tenderly, sometimes lustily passionate.

He never pressed her for a verbal commitment, although she had a feeling that he took it for granted in a sense. He seemed to understand her better than she did herself. Rebel had ceased being surprised at questions answered before they were asked, accepting that as on a par with this puzzling situation.

By Tuesday night, Rebel had come to several private decisions and conclusions. And the result of those was that she would have to make a trip into Casper. Alone.

"Donovan?"

"Hmm?"

"Look at me when I'm talking to you."

"I was contemplating your navel."

"I noticed. Did you find the secrets of the universe?"

"No. I just got dizzy."

Rebel resolutely pulled up the covers. "Get out from under there and pay attention to me."

Donovan emerged from the covers. "I *was* paying attention to you. Strict attention. Undivided attention." He began to languidly explore the flesh of her throat.

"Donovan..." Rebel locked her fingers in his thick hair and had to clear her throat before intelligible words would emerge. "I called the heliport today."

The dark head lifted abruptly, startled violet eyes staring into hers. "You did? Why?" His voice was careful.

"I'm going into Casper tomorrow."

"Why?" he repeated.

Gently, she said, "Donovan, I didn't plan on staying this long. I have some shopping to do."

"I'll go with you," he said rather hastily.

Still more gently, she said, "You have to stay here and work on Astaire. Remember? The land? The reason we're here?"

He just stared at her.

"Afraid I'll slip my leash?" she asked sardonically.

"I'm afraid you'll catch the first mule train back to Dallas," he said frankly.

"Oh, no. I'm going to see this thing through. Observe the final curtain, so to speak."

Donovan looked with some suspicion at her bland expression. "I can still go with you," he said at last. "Astaire mentioned some calls he needed to make in the morning, so..."

Rebel shook her head slowly.

"Pulling rank, boss?'

"Oh, can I still do that?" she asked with mock surprise.

"Rebel, you know..."

Yes, she knew. She knew that Donovan had chosen to follow her, even though he was innately a leader himself. Knowing him better than she had before, Rebel no longer questioned his willingness to work for her, to take her orders. He followed because he wanted to, and that implied a strength she found intriguing.

Unwilling to enter into a discussion about that right now, and still seeking the pieces of her puzzle, she cut him off with a sudden change of subject.

"Tell me something. Why did you tell Carson that I was allergic to shellfish?"

"Because you are."

"Yes, but how did you know that? I only found out myself a few months ago." She watched the startled, bemused flicker in his violet eyes and tried once again to figure out what it meant.

"You must have mentioned it," he said finally.

She shook her head firmly. "No. The subject never came up."

"Then Marc must have mentioned it."

"He doesn't know."

Impatiently, Donovan said, "Then it was Bessie. Or you mentioned it and just don't remember it. Or something."

"Right. Or something." That part of Rebel's puzzle was still empty. The pieces were flitting elusively through her mind, and she hadn't been able to grasp them yet. But she would.

"Are we going to talk all night?" he demanded.

Rebel wound her arms around his neck with a smile. "Perish the thought," she murmured.

The helicopter Rebel had rented picked her up at the lodge the next morning and flew her directly to Casper. She kept her eyes resolutely up for most of the trip, not daring to look down until she had to get out of the craft.

Donovan had made one last attempt to convince her to allow him to come along with her. She had resisted firmly, although she still felt a bit weak-kneed when she thought about his blandishments.

She got a taxi at the airport and was driven to a large shopping center that looked promising. For a while she simply wandered, picking up a few odds and ends she needed.

Then she located a phone booth and placed a collect call to her apartment in Dallas. She was supposed to be joining her parents in Paris for Christmas, and something told her that she'd better be prepared to forgo that trip. It was beginning to look as if she'd be in the Bighorn Mountains for the holiday. She had to at least alert Bessie.

Puzzlement reigned, though, as she listened to the operator identify the caller, get permission to reverse the charges, and then get off the line.

"Dad? What are you doing in Dallas?"

"Oh, your mother had a hankering to spend the holidays in the States," the elder Sinclair told his daughter in an offhand voice. "When're you coming home?"

"That's why I called." Rebel felt a little uncomfortable, but she wasn't quite sure why. "It looks like I may be stuck here for a while."

"Lennox being troublesome?" Marc asked sympathetically.

"Not really, but he just won't be pinned down. It may take another week to close the deal."

"It's a shame for you to miss Christmas," her father said with a curious lack of regret in his voice. "Your mother and I will be disappointed if you don't make it home. But—I know—business comes first."

Rebel held the receiver several inches from her ear and stared at it for a moment. Then she got back on the line. "Is Mom there? Can I talk to her?"

"Sorry, honey, she's out shopping. You know your mother; she always waits until the last minute."

"I suppose Bessie's with her?"

"Sure is. They were out at dawn and left me to sleep in."

"Oh." Rebel frowned at the stream of holiday shoppers flowing past her. "Well, give them both my love and tell them I'll be home as soon as possible."

"I will, honey. You take care, and we'll see you soon."

"All right. 'Bye, Dad."

"'Bye."

Rebel hung up the phone slowly, continuing to stare at the people rushing past. Her father, she realized, had seemed awfully anxious not to prolong the conversation. That hurt a little. But what really hurt was that he hadn't seemed at all upset by the possibility of her missing their traditional family Christmas.

Frowning, Rebel bent to pick up her shopping bag and joined the throng. Pushing the brief conversation from her mind, she went to find a restaurant and have lunch.

After lunch, she wandered again, something definite in mind now. It was, in fact, the entire point of this trip into town. She was looking for something special, and she had to visit three jewelry stores before she finally found it.

Luck or fate was with her; it was exactly what she wanted. The small package was carefully and gaily wrapped in the store, and she hid it in the bottom of her shopping bag before leaving.

She wandered for a bit longer. After passing three phones in the mall and looking thoughtfully at each of them, Rebel finally gave in to the urge and placed another call—again, to Dallas. Ordinarily she wouldn't have even thought of checking up on Donovan...but she had to know.

Josh was surprised by her question. Except for one routine call to make certain that everything was all right at the office, he hadn't heard from Donovan. Orders? No, no orders in regard to Lennox, except to ask for Donovan rather than Rebel if he needed to call the lodge for anything. And, by the way, everything was fine at the office.

Rebel hung up the phone slowly. "You forgot to cover that base, Donovan," she murmured to herself.

The conversation she had overheard days before now assumed new importance. Whom had Donovan talked to on the phone that day? He'd said, "He's still in Denver," and to her mind that meant that he hadn't been speaking to Astaire. Who, then? And what about? He'd talked of something upsetting airline schedules all over the world. He'd said, "Well, wouldn't you smell a rat?" He'd said that timing was important. That someone was "blindly unsuspecting." That it was important to him.

It? What was *it?*

Rebel found an unoccupied wooden bench in the mall and sat down to think. Donovan and Astaire were in cahoots—that much she was sure of. And she had the peculiar feeling that this was another one of those conspiracies entered into for her own good.

For a moment she was sorely tempted to dig the buried package out of her bag and dump it into the fountain a few yards away. But she didn't. *That* decision had been made, and nothing short of sheer betrayal would alter it. And the possibility of Donovan's being after her company had long since been banished.

But what was the point? Why keep up the tenuous fiction of bargaining for that property? And why keep her in the dark about whatever was going on?

The pieces of her puzzle were falling into place, but the overall picture *still* didn't make sense.

It was, Rebel decided irritably, like waiting for the jaws of a trap to slam shut.

Sighing, she got up to go hunting a taxi. She'd go back to the lodge and confront Donovan. He'd talked about boxing the shadows of her past; she had no intention of boxing the shadows of his present. One way or another, she was going to find out what lengths his devious mind had gone to. And if she found out—as she strongly suspected—that he'd simply wanted to get her alone and away from the office . . .

Well, she could accept that. What woman wouldn't? It was flattering, and it made her smile the same way she'd smiled when she had watched him decorating a Christmas tree in secret.

The trip back to the lodge was uneventful. She was so wrapped up in her thoughts, in fact, that the helicopter ride didn't bother her at all. She even managed a cheery wave to the pilot as the small craft lifted off one of the pads at the lodge.

Carson met her at the door with the information that Mr. Knight and Mr. Lennox were in the library, in the Early American wing. Rebel merely nodded and allowed the butler to take her coat, purse, and shopping bag, asking him politely to put the bag in the closet in her bedroom. Being Carson, he immediately went to do so.

Rebel wandered in search of the library, passing the kitchen en route and puzzled by the loud activity going on in there. It sounded, she thought, as though they were getting ready to feed an army. She wondered if Astaire's family was coming for the holidays after all.

That thought didn't remain long in her mind, because she reached the door of the library. It was slightly open, and she paused instinctively when she heard two male voices. It came to her that she could make a career out of overhearing conversations not meant for her ears. But she didn't announce her presence.

"That's slander, my boy. Character assasination. No wonder the poor girl gave me such a look when I finally showed up."

"It served its purpose." Donovan's voice was amused.

Astaire snorted. "Well, it'll serve you right if she takes the first carrier pigeon back to Texas when she finds out what you've done. Most women would."

"Rebel isn't most women."

"For your sake, I hope not. Couldn't you have found a simpler way of convincing her that you loved her? You get her up here on the flimsiest of pretenses, keep her here for days while we pretend to argue about land she could have for the asking, go to great lengths to 'arrange' things when she isn't looking . . . How long do you expect to keep this up?"

"As long as necessary."

"Sure. And from what I've seen and heard of her, when you paint her into a corner and announce your engagement, she'll probably hit you in the face with the paintbrush."

"Probably." Donovan chuckled. "Look, I want her to decide for herself that I'm not after that damned company. Once she's made up her mind about that, I'll tell her everything."

"Better hope that's soon. Damon's chewing nails; he says he's going to shoot you for keeping him in Denver all this time."

"If he comes up here before I've explained him, I'll shoot *him*. If Rebel gets a look at him, I'm finished."

"What about when she gets a look at the rest? You've got everyone heading this way; they'll start rolling in tomorrow. It won't take Damon to point out the family resemblance, you know; your mother and I look like twins."

"I know, I know."

"You'd better work fast, my boy."

"Tell me about it." Donovan sighed. "I didn't even know until we got up here that I'd have a chance with Rebel. And I sure wasn't certain I could keep her here until Christmas. Still, it seemed the best way."

"Because you want to be loved for yourself."

"Don't point out that I'm being idealistic; I know that."

Astaire laughed suddenly. "You know, for two people who want exactly the same thing—to be loved for themselves—you've managed to hellishly complicate the situation."

"That has occurred to me."

While both men laughed, Rebel crept away silently, having heard all she wanted to hear. She made her way back to the greatroom. Crossing to the bar, she poured herself a snifter of brandy—a large snifter—and began to pace. The first gulp of liquor burned all the way down. The second gulp followed the well-blazed trail and scalded only slightly. The third gulp pleasantly warmed.

The puzzle was assembling itself in her mind—be it ever so increasingly fuzzy a mind—and the picture justifiably roused her temper.

The whole thing had been a plot! Donovan's plot. No wonder Carson and the rest of the staff had backed him up in his ridiculous wooing—he'd probably spent half his childhood at this lodge!

Unscrupulous, conniving, deceitful—aahhh! She'd kill him. With great pleasure and malice aforethought. She'd boil him in oil and dangle him from a turret. Turret? No . . . from the point of one of the A-frames.

No wonder she'd felt that Astaire looked familiar—there was a definite, although elusive, resemblance to Donovan. And the painting missing from that wall was probably a family portrait—with Donovan squarely in the middle.

Damn the man! Making her agonize over whether it was she or the company he wanted, when all the time his family could have bought and sold Sinclair Hotels a dozen times over. It just wasn't fair!

She didn't let herself consider the fact that Donovan had apparently wanted only what she did herself—to be trusted and loved until nothing else was important. That was not the point. Not at the moment. She was mad, and it felt good to be mad, and good to have something definite to be mad *about*.

Damn the man. Getting her into helicopters and hanging mistletoe and decorating Christmas trees and making love to her until she couldn't think and reading her mind when she *could*, and—

Reading her mind?

The fanciful thought skittered through her mind and screeched to a halt. She sat down rather abruptly and tried to focus her eyes on the opposite wall.

Psychic? Oh, no—ridiculous! That was a weird thought. A definitely weird and unnerving thought. Still . . .

She remembered the past six months. Her seemingly uncanny affinity with Donovan—or his with her. All the things she'd not had to tell him. His ability to anticipate her wishes, to see what she had in mind before she was certain herself.

And then there was this fateful trip. The moment on the jet when she had *seen* him for the first time—and he had realized it. The small things: questions answered before they were asked; his telling her where the tapes were when he'd been lying there with his eyes shut and couldn't have known that was what she had in mind; the very tree she'd fallen in love with selected and decorated in secret; his knowing she was allergic to shellfish.

Then came the clincher—and Rebel was appalled that she hadn't realized it sooner.

The night he had tried to convince her that he had no interest in the company, she had left him believing that he hadn't been successful. She had seen the defeat on his face. But then she had paced and wrestled with herself and gone out into the sitting room and dreamed of a lover. And he had come to her.

Rebel rather hastily got to her feet and poured more brandy. It had a reasonable explanation—all of it. She did *not* believe in ESP and mental telepathy and precognition . . . it hadn't been proven yet, after all. But wouldn't it be just like the man to have something like that up his sleeve!

This time Rebel took the bottle back with her to the chair. She'd get completely blotto, and then she'd mop up the floor with Donovan. And tomorrow she'd tie her head on with a piece of string or something, call the heliport and rent another damned copter, and go back to Dallas.

By the time Donovan and Astaire came into the great-room about an hour later, Rebel could have picked a fight with a saint.

"I want to talk to you!" she announced clearly, rising to her feel with wonderful balance and pointing one of the fingers not wrapped around the snifter at him.

The two men, she noticed with mental clarity, looked as though they were about be confronted by a volcanic eruption. It was a vastly pleasing thought, since either of them would make two of her.

"Sure." Donovan came toward her rather carefully.

Astaire made haste to vacate the battleground. "You two want to be alone, I'm sure—"

Rebel leaned sideways, coming perilously close to tipping over. "Don't rush off, *Uncle* Astaire," she said gently, peering past the bulk that was Donovan. "That is who you are, isn't it?"

"Uh-oh," Donovan murmured with resignation.

"I'm too old for this," Astaire said plaintively. "If you'll excuse me, I'll—uh—go check on dinner."

"Don't bother." Rebel walked cautiously around the coffee table, reasoning that battles took space and she didn't want to be trapped beside the couch. Very sweetly she told them, "I've already spoken to the cook. He will shortly serve up two man-sized portions of *hemlock!*"

While Astaire made himself scarce, Donovan murmured, "You've been drinking."

Rebel toasted him with her nearly empty snifter. "I would have been disappointed if you hadn't noticed."

"We'll talk about this tomorrow—"

"We'll talk about it *now!* Would you like to try to explain this web of lies you've got me tangled in?"

"Rebel—"

She pursued her prey relentlessly. "You lied about Astaire's being a rake; you lied about his prejudice against women executives. You lied by—by implication when you didn't tell me he was your uncle—"

"How did you find out?" he interrupted.

Rebel drew herself up and glared at him. "I eaves-dropped," she announced defiantly. "When you were in the library."

Donovan sighed. "We didn't hear the helicopter."

"Well, lucky for me! Otherwise, you might never have let me in on the secret."

"Rebel, that was only because—"

"And another thing!" she interrupted, wanting to air all her grievances before he could somehow manage to outgun her yet again. "You've been reading my mind! That's an invasion of privacy, and I'm going to *sue!*"

"They'd throw it out of court," he murmured, a tremor of mirth in his deep voice.

"If you think I'm going to marry a man who knows what I'm thinking before *I* know what I'm thinking, you're crazy!"

"You have to marry me," he said calmly. "We're going to make the announcement at the party. I've disrupted airline schedules all over the world to get everyone here."

Rebel blinked at him. "What party?" she asked, pieces of the puzzle still busily falling into place and confusing her.

"The Christmas party," Donovan told her gently. "Both our families will be here."

"Here?" Some part of Rebel's mind felt relief as she realized that *that* was why her father hadn't sounded disappointed at the unlikelihood of her attending the traditional family Christmas. But the full import of his statement didn't sink in for a moment. "Who's Damon?" she demanded abruptly, her wayward mind latching onto the vaguely puzzling name.

"My cousin. He's coming to the party, too."

"Astaire's son?" she hazarded.

"Bingo," he murmured. "You're not as tipsy as I thought."

"I am not tipsy," she announced with tipsy dignity. She made a horizon-sweeping gesture with her free hand. "I'm blotto."

"It's nice to know you can lose control occasionally," Donovan observed musingly. "I mean, out of bed and with your clothes on."

Rebel had to try twice before the words would emerge. "Ohhh—that was a low blow!"

"Sorry," he murmured.

Rebel glared at him owlishly for a moment, and then the needle dropped into its proper track. "Party. What's this about a party?"

"A Christmas party," he repeated patiently. "And an engagement party. Both our families will be here."

"All your daunting sisters?" she asked uneasily.

"All my daunting sisters. And my parents. Assorted in-laws, nieces, nephews, cousins—the Lennox side of the family, you know. And your parents, and Bessie."

Rebel could feel the horror overtaking her face, and Donovan choked on a laugh.

"Am I fired, boss?"

"Fired? *Killing's* too good for you! Donovan," she wailed, "how could you do this to me?"

"I admit it's a little underhanded, but—"

"It's the most infamous, deceitful—" Shock went a long way toward dispersing the mists of brandy. She set the snifter down carefully on the coffee table and then straightened. Glaring at the fiend, she said with vast politeness, "Would you mind very much telling me exactly who your family is?"

He obviously knew what she wanted to know—and just as obviously wished he didn't have to tell her.

"Ever hear of the Knoxx Group?" he asked casually.

"Well, of course I have. It's a worldwide conglomerate." She was pleased that the difficult word emerged correctly.

"That's the family," he murmured. "Dad and Astaire merged their companies forty years ago. Over the years, the family grew and scattered to take care of the expanding businesses. So now we have diversified companies all over the world."

Rebel wanted to sit down, but she forced her knees to lock and continue to support her. "And you work for me," she said dazedly. "A worldwide conglomerate as your birthright, and you work for me."

"I told you I wasn't interested in power," he pointed out.

Rebel stared at him as the last piece of the puzzle dropped into place. Now the picture made sense.

Donovan sighed. "I never wanted to have much to do with the business, and Dad—thankfully—understood. But I did want to help out without actually getting into the rat race myself. So for about ten years I acted as a sort of troubleshooter for Knoxx. I traveled all over the world—I told you that. I just didn't tell you why.

"By the time I met you, I was ready to settle down. The last thing I wanted was an executive position, but I didn't have much choice. So I joined Sinclair."

"Dad knew," she murmured.

"Of course. I was very honest with Marc."

It was a poor choice of words. Rebel didn't need the fumes of brandy this time. She got mad all by herself.

"You swine!" she yelled in a fine imitation of Vesuvius. "Do you know what you put me through? Do you know how I agonized over the possibility that you could be after the company? That nearly drove me crazy!"

"Rebel—"

"And do you know the worst part? I stopped caring whether you were after the company or not! I would have handed the damned thing to you on a plate! And do you know what that did to my self-respect? Can you possibly guess?"

He stepped toward her quickly, a sudden glow in his eyes. "Rebel, are you saying—?"

"I'm saying that I love you, dammit, and you tricked me!" she snarled wrathfully.

Immediately, she was caught in a bone-crushing bear hug. Hard lips found hers in a bruising, possessive kiss. "Thank God," he muttered against her mouth. He literally picked her up and swung her in a happy circle, which did absolutely nothing to restore her brandy-and-kiss-disordered senses.

And then he laughed, resting his forehead against hers and gazing down at her with tender eyes. "Oh, honey, I'll treasure that declaration all the days of our lives!"

"I'm still mad at you," she managed weakly.

"That's all right," he said comfortingly. "You're magnificent when you're angry. And I deserve it."

"You certainly do," she said promptly, swaying slightly as he set her back on her feet.

Donovan put an arm around her and began leading her from the room. "Let's get some food into you to balance the brandy," he said wryly. "You will definitely have a head tomorrow."

"Somebody else's," she agreed, wondering where the anger had gone.

He stopped in the archway. "Tell me again."

Rebel looked up into shining violet eyes and felt her whole face soften with the glow of a love acknowledged at long last. "I love you," she whispered.

"And I love you," he murmured, bending to kiss her tenderly.

He was taking advantage of the mistletoe above them. Again.

* * *

Rebel knew that, even now, Donovan couldn't be sure
that she had made her decision before finding out who
he really was. Being Donovan, he had accepted what
she'd said. But he couldn't be *sure*.

The proof was in a shopping bag in her closet. And
at an appropriate moment, she'd give it to him. But not
just yet. She intended to let *him* be uncertain for a while.

Food cleared more of the cobwebs from her mind,
and she managed to resurrect her glare during dinner.
He didn't have to have everything his own way, after
all. And she *was* mad.

She kept glaring until the lights went out in their
bedroom.

Then he wooed her.

Chapter 9

REBEL AWOKE THE next morning with someone else's head, and she hated every living thing. Donovan didn't waste time or effort in trying to convince her that she would actually get better; he simply inserted her efficiently into a steaming hot bath and met her occasional fading moans with spurious sympathy.

Rebel knew that she was dying, and she intended to make quite a lot of noise about it. She had never been one to suffer in silence. No one in the long and eventful history of mankind, she thought with some vague satisfaction, had suffered as much as she was suffering now.

Added to her agony was the unmercifully vivid memory of how she had acted the day before. She was by no means ashamed of her temper, nor did she regret the brandy-induced scene with Donovan. It had cleared up several puzzling matters after all. But she hated losing control of herself, and announcing her love to Donovan with a wrathful snarl had not been the way she had planned it.

Turning her head carefully and literally hearing the creak of rusty hinges, she glowered over at the vanity, where Donovan was busy shaving. "Tell me it didn't happen," she requested faintly. "Tell me that I didn't hear you announce that an entire battalion of your relatives is arriving today."

"Sorry, love." He sent a look brimful of laughter her way. "It did happen. And they are coming."

"Donovan, I am going to kill you. Slowly, and taking great care to prolong your agony, I am going to kill you." She rested her head carefully on the lip of the tub and closed her eyes. "And after that, I'm going to climb this mountain and, like that prospector, I'm never coming down again."

"The aspirin should start working any minute now," he told her consolingly.

"You think it's just the hangover, but it isn't. You have grossly deceived me all along, and I'm going to get you for that. I will turn into six kinds of a shrew and make your life hideous. Are you listening to this?"

"No, sweetheart, I'm shaving."

"Donovan, would you for once—just once—get mad and yell back at me?"

"In your condition? It'd kill you."

"Well, when I'm better, you'd better yell at me."

"What is this masochistic desire to feel my anger?"

"It isn't masochistic at all. It's just that if you don't get mad, I'll live in terror of hearing the other shoe drop."

"There's a crazy kind of logic in that," he observed thoughtfully.

Rebel opened her eyes long enough to send him a

pained stare. "Tell me again who's coming. Then I can drown myself."

"Everyone's coming."

"Can you at least give me a *number?*"

"Well, to be honest, I've kinda lost count. I can give you a reasonable estimate of the Knight clan, but the Lennox clan seems to sprout like weeds. Damon isn't married, but Astaire had eight daughters, and they have innumerable kids—"

Awed, she murmured, "Girls must run in your family."

"They do," he told her cheerfully. "And it's odd when you think about it. Since sex is determined by the male, you'd think my sisters could have logically expected to have a roughly even number of boys. But between the six of them, there are only two boys: Kelly and Geneva each have one. And the boys are always dark; the girls tend to get the red hair."

Rebel decided that the aspirin was beginning to take effect; she was fascinated by this. "Tell me more."

Donovan came over to sit on the edge of the tub, a towel knotted around his lean waist. "I'm afraid it'll make you take to your heels," he said wryly.

"If I haven't run by now, I won't. I seem to have lost my sanity somewhere along the way." Her voice was bemused.

"That's the second-nicest thing you've ever said to me, love." He leaned over to kiss her briefly, then straightened. "What do you want to know?"

"I think I have a fair grasp on the Knight clan; how about the Lennox side? Do you have uncles other than Astaire?"

"No, but I have six aunts. They all have children and some grandchildren—mostly girls. At last count, I think there were three boys other than Damon, all dark."

Rebel made a stab at mental multiplication but gave

up very quickly. "My God," she murmured faintly. Backing up a bit, and not sure she wanted to hear the answer, she said, "Your father. He can't be an only child."

"One of six. The rest—"

"Don't tell me. Girls."

"Bingo."

Rebel thought it was no wonder Donovan didn't have a chauvinistic bone in his body. If he'd had any notions of sexual inequality, the girls in his family would have blasted them out of existence at an early age. "I wonder why the boys are all dark," she murmured absently. "Those Indians in the family history you mentioned?"

"That's our theory. By the way, the girls tend to marry young, but not the boys."

She stared at him. "All these people are coming up here?"

He nodded cheerfully. "Yep."

"Donovan, I am going to kill you . . ."

She was still repeating those same words as she peered around Donovan and out one of the front windows, trying to get a look at the suddenly busy helipads. "Donovan, I am going to kill you. Is that a troop carrier, for God's sake?"

"It pretty much has to be, don't you think?"

"Oh, Lord—that has to be your father. *Damn*, I'm going to kill you. Why didn't you warn me? And why didn't you let me out of that bathtub in time to at least fix my hair—"

"You look beautiful. And I happen to love your hair down. Will you stop worrying? They'll love you."

Rebel nervously smoothed her denim-clad thighs. "I should have worn a dress. Why didn't you let me wear a dress?" She would have felt more sure of herself confronting the army of a hostile nation.

"Because you look cute as a button in jeans."

"I've never seen so many redheaded people in my life!"

She didn't have a chance to say much of anything else before the deluge began—and went on all afternoon. At some point she began to feel that she was looking at a film rushing past, with an occasional still-frame stopping the motion temporarily. It was those moments she remembered.

"Mom, Dad, this is Rebel."

"So this is the lady you've been moving heaven and earth for, eh, son?" Randall Knight was as tall and upright as his son, although age had turned his black hair silver and sapped the muscles from his thin frame. But the years had done nothing to dim the mischief in his violet eyes. "Well, she looks like she's worth it."

"Don't tease the poor girl, Randall—can't you see she's bewildered by all of us? You should be ashamed, Donovan! Welcome to the family, my dear." Leslie Knight was as upright and very nearly as tall as her husband, silver-haired and blue-eyed. And both she and her husband gave Rebel a warm and welcoming hug.

"And this is Geneva."

"Well, thank God, not another redhead! Maybe we can have a few nicely neutral kids in the family instead of carrot-tops or Indians!" Geneva topped the six-foot mark and moved with the brisk determination of someone who couldn't bear to be still.

Shaking hand with Donovan's brother-in-law Adam, Rebel felt duty-bound to mention the unlikelihood of that. "My father's a redhead," she pointed out meekly. "And I think there are a few more on the family tree . . ."

"Oh, God! Will this redheaded curse never be broken?"

"You're blocking traffic, Gen. Move aside and let the rest of the army in."

"Donovan, you're a snake. If you weren't my only brother, and if I hadn't been *insatiably* curious to find out what kind of woman had finally managed to catch you—"

"Who caught who?" Rebel mumbled involuntarily.

"Whom," Geneva corrected automatically, and then immediately completed her sentence. "—I never would have dropped everything in Japan and come rushing out here on that excuse for a plane—"

"Adam, can you do something with her? Preferably take her into the greatroom and gag her?"

"Come along, darling."

"That pilot should be ashamed of himself..."

"Charley, Rick, this is Rebel."

Rebel looked at the slender, auburn-haired woman who was perhaps five-ten in her stocking feet, and said weakly, "They call you half-pint?"

"Well, Rick does—isn't it terrible of him? My, how pretty you are! And so tiny! I met your father; he's so sweet. And your mother's just lovely. Donovan, you look so happy! I'm so glad for both of you. Three children at least, and *maybe* a boy..."

Still reeling under the shock of being called tiny, Rebel shook hands with Rick and watched as he followed the wife who had drifted away on a wave of half-sentences and fragments.

"Marc, Vanessa—glad you could make it. Vanessa, you look as lovely as usual."

"Flatterer. Merry Christmas, darling! How are you holding up?"

"Mom, how could you let him do this to me?"

"Well, darling, I didn't have much to say about it, you know. Bessie, *will* you stop hovering over that box? It doesn't contain the crown jewels!"

"It's got my cake in it, and that's more valuable."
Black eyes snapped with a peculiar sort of Latin satisfaction as Bessie took in the picture of Rebel leaning
somewhat weakly against Donovan. "Took you long
enough!" she announced, and she sailed off to the kitchen
with her carefully baked cake.

Rebel met her father's laughing blue eyes resignedly.
"Hi, Dad."

"Merry Christmas, honey," he chuckled in response.

The onslaught continued. Rebel rapidly lost count of
the adults and didn't even try to keep track of the younger
generations. It was like being hit in the face with a tidal
wave of good wishes and loud voices, and once Rebel
recovered from the initial shock and began to relax, she
found herself enjoying it.

The huge lodge, so empty until now, was packed to overflowing with people ranging in age from six months to
their mid-seventies. Everyone was warm and welcoming
to Rebel. They were a close and affectionate family, cheerfully insulting one another but never with malice. The whole
lodge fairly throbbed with them.

And enough redheads to start their own country. No
redheaded boys, though. Not a single one among the
younger generations.

"Rebel, this is Damon."

She looked up into twinkling, clear blue eyes and
murmured involuntarily, "Well, no wonder you didn't
want him here."

Damon Lennox was very nearly a carbon copy of
Donovan. The same size, the same black hair silvered
at the temples, uncannily similar features. Except for the
blue eyes. One look at him, and she would have instantly
known the two men were related.

With a laugh, Damon said, "I was ready to shoot him

for keeping me in Denver, but I see now that it was worth it."

Even the voice was nearly identical.

"Hands off, cousin," Donovan warned lightly. "She's taken."

"Pity," Damon murmured, eyes twinkling as he went to join the throng.

The still-frame image that Rebel would cherish for years she literally stumbled on the next day. Passing by one of the lounges in search of her missing fiancé, she glanced through the doorway and stopped in her tracks, a hand over her mouth to halt the giggle.

Carson, not a hair out of place or a shred of dignity lost, was on his hands and knees on the floor. On his back were two tiny copper-haired girls who periodically shrieked, "Horsey!" in unison.

Standing in front of the butler, nose-to-nose and peering solemnly, was a black-haired boy of perhaps four. "Cookie," he said firmly. "Want a cookie."

"May I have a cookie," Carson corrected austerely.

The child thought it over. "May I have a cookie," he finally repeated carefully. "Now."

Rebel retreated hastily, giggling. When she ran Donovan down in the greatroom, she related the story with a laugh. Donovan shared her amusement but wasn't at all surprised. He told her gravely that he had learned manners from the butler at about the same age.

Having been indecently rushed for nearly two weeks and practically railroaded into her engagement, Rebel planned Christmas Eve carefully. Knowing full well that the next day would be a day of noise and confusion after Santa's visit, she wanted this night to be a special one for her and Donovan alone.

So when Donovan came into their sitting room slightly

before midnight, having been kept occupied by both her father and his at her request, she was ready.

The champagne was icing in its silver bucket, near at hand. A fire blazed cheerfully in the hearth. Pillows were piled on the white fur rug in front of the fire. And Rebel reclined against the pillows, her blue satin-and-lace nightgown shimmering in the fire's shifting glow.

She looked up as he entered the room, watching him as he halted for a moment and then reached back to lock the door.

"You're reading my mind again," she murmured.

"Don't be ridiculous." He came toward her, handsome and devilish in his stark black shirt and slacks, violet eyes glowing. "That would be impossible."

"Sure it would."

"Really."

"Uh-huh. Once more with feeling."

"Are we going to talk about impossible things all night?" he demanded, kicking off his shoes and sinking down beside her.

"And cabbages and kings," she murmured. "I thought you said that nothing was impossible?"

"Don't fling my own words back at me."

Rebel calmly pushed the champagne bucket his way when he would have reached for her. "Why don't we drink a toast to Christmas," she suggested limpidly, producing two hollow-stemmed glasses and smiling sweetly at him.

Donovan sighed and began working on the bottle. "If that's what you want. But I don't need champagne . . . I've got you."

Rebel smiled but said nothing, waiting until the cork had popped and bubbly liquid filled both glasses. Then she lifted her glass and said softly, "To Christmas."

His glass touched hers lightly. "To fifty more Christmas toasts made together," he responded firmly.

The toast was duly drunk, and then Donovan reached into his pocket and drew out a small black velvet box. Setting aside his glass, he opened the box to reveal a beautiful sapphire engagement ring. "To make it official. I've been carrying this around with me for months." He slid the ring carefully onto the proper finger. "Merry Christmas, darling."

Rebel stared at the glittering ring and swallowed hard. "It's lovely." Her smile turned teasing. "I haven't actually heard a proposal, you know. Lots of statements and commands, but not a single very simple question."

Donovan smiled and lifted her hand to his lips, kissing it gently. "I've loved you for a very long time," he said quietly, gazing into her eyes, his own flaring with a savagely simple feeling. "I used to watch you in the office when you weren't looking. So close . . . and so far away. We'd be working at your apartment and you'd sit down beside me on the couch—and I had to fight every instinct screaming to grab you.

"After one of those twelve-hour days topped off by an interminable board meeting, you always looked so tired. I wanted to take you in my arms, to share some of the burden you were so determined to bear alone. But you wouldn't let me."

He sighed heavily. "So I plotted and I schemed—and I lied to you. I created a problem where none existed, building it around that land—land that I could have gotten for you with a phone call. I had to get you away from the office; I had to somehow break through that chrysalis you'd wrapped yourself in.

"I knew that I was taking a chance. God, I knew. And when you told me about your husband and what he'd done to you, I understood how hard it would be to convince you that it was you I wanted and not the company. The truth would have convinced you—the truth about my family, I mean. But I wanted you to trust me and believe in me. So I kept trying to convince you."

He paused again, and Rebel sensed that he wanted to say something more, that he wanted to be certain she had made up her mind about his motives before finding out the truth about his family. But he didn't question her.

"Rebel, I love you with everything inside of me. I want to spend the rest of my life with you. Will you marry me?"

Rebel couldn't answer him with words. Silently, she reached behind the pillows and pulled out a small, gaily wrapped box, handing it to him and feeling suddenly shy.

Donovan looked at the package and then at her, puzzled but smiling. "Is this your answer?"

She nodded. "I got it that day I went to Casper."

Beginning to unwrap the box, Donovan looked up at her suddenly, and she could see the realization in his eyes. After a moment, he somewhat hastily tore the colorful paper away and opened the box. She saw a tremor in the long fingers as he slowly lifted her gift from its box, and that evidence of deep emotion moved her almost unbearably.

"Every lord of the castle should have one," she said shakily.

Silently, Donovan slipped the fine golden chain over his head, looking down for a moment at the exquisitely crafted gold key resting in the palm of his hand. "Given freely," he murmured huskily.

"Given freely... and with all my love. I love you, Donovan. I've known that since the night I opened my bedroom door and saw you decorating a Christmas tree in secret."

He reached out to frame her face in his hands, looking

at her as though at the secrets of the universe. "You realized that I wasn't interested in the company—that I loved you."

"More than that." She fumbled for the explanation that was only now beginning to crystalize in her mind. "Donovan, when I found out that Jud had only wanted the company, something happened. The company was never important to me until then. But after that, I felt— in a crazy way—that I had to prove my ability to master what had very nearly destroyed me. If I could control it, it wouldn't be a threat to me any longer. I didn't blame Jud for what had happened—I blamed the company. So I set out to master it.

"And then we came up here. I was away from the company; I could see it—and myself—clearly for the first time in years. And listening to you talk about it put the company in perspective for me. It is just a business, just a small cog in a huge wheel. It didn't ruin my marriage—Jud did.

"The company doesn't matter anymore. It stopped being the most important thing in my life the first time I looked at you ... and *saw* you. It isn't your rival any more than it's mine."

Donovan pulled her fiercely into his arms, holding her tightly for a long moment. "Thank God," he muttered. "I was afraid that company would always stand between us."

"Oh, no," she murmured, sliding her arms up around his neck and smiling tenderly into his shining eyes. "Who needs a company? I've got you."

"You certainly have ..." Impatiently, he pushed aside the silver bucket, their glasses, and the empty jeweler's boxes and pulled her down into the furry softness of the white rug. "And I'll never let you get away from me now."

Happily absorbing the weight of him, Rebel blindly

sought the buttons of his shirt as his mouth found hers. The ember flared to new and blazing life within her, and need coursed through her body like molten lava as tongues met in a hungry duel.

His shirt was cast aside, falling unnoticed to provide a black dustcover for the champagne bucket. Her gown and the remainder of his clothing swiftly followed.

"You're so beautiful," he whispered, lips searching out the hollows of her throat, hands shaping willing flesh. "So exciting. I'll never get enough of you!"

"I have a lot to make up for," she murmured throatily, her fingers tangled in his thick black hair as she thought of the year he had waited patiently.

"No." He pressed warm kisses over her face. "That wasn't your fault; you couldn't help it. And the wait was worth it, love."

But Rebel understood now the strain of his patient wait. And she wanted to make it up to him somehow. Fiercely, she pushed against his shoulders until he rolled onto his back. Half lying against his side, she eagerly explored his neck and shoulders with her lips.

"On the other hand," he rasped, "if you feel obligated . . ."

Rebel nearly giggled, but passion swiftly pushed the laughter aside. She used her teeth and tongue to torment and then soothe, experimentally tasting his flesh and finding the sensation addictive. Her mouth continued to search, finding the flat male nipples and teasing them with a flicking tongue. His groan of pleasure spurred her on, and she only dimly noticed that his hands were far from still, threading through her hair, stroking her back.

She followed the narrowing trail of black hair down over his flat belly until she reached the throbbing desire he felt for her. She felt him jerk involuntarily as she touched him, held him, and a primitive and loving hunger enveloped her.

Donovan groaned harshly, a shudder shaking his strong body. "Rebel! Honey, you're driving me out of my mind!"

Some distant part of Rebel's mind silently acknowledged that she wanted to do just that. She wanted controls splintered, restraint lost. The need in her was beyond thought, beyond reason. She wanted layers of civilization stripped away, leaving only the primitive bonding of man and woman.

And that hunger drove her relentlessly. She tormented, teased, incited, using the knowledge these past days with him had given her. She found feminine instincts within her she had not known existed. She became woman incarnate.

And Donovan wasn't about to resist. He lifted her back up into his arms frantically. The strength of him was almost bruising now, and Rebel gloried in every moment of it. She met strength with strength, bending without breaking to the savage need she had kindled to life within him.

Lips clashed in a firestorm of desire, hands caressed with blind urgency. Time tunneled, focused on an eternal second, and then ground to a halt.

Their joining was explosive, devastating in its intensity. They loved and fought like the primitive beings this moment had made them. Both taking, both giving, merging in a driven effort to share one body, one soul.

And for one shattering moment they did just that, two souls clinging in an instinctive recognition of affinity.

"Donovan!"

"Rebel . . ."

Rebel decided she was never going to move again if she could possibly avoid it. She'd just lie here on this fur rug in front of a crackling fire and in Donovan's arms. The world could go on without her.

"Good Lord," Donovan murmured, his voice drained and more than a bit awed. "Did I dream that?"

Rebel stirred slightly, eyes closed and an extremely feminine smile on her face. "You've been branded, milord," she told him softly. "Now you're all mine."

"It wasn't just your sense of obligation, then?"

"Not really. Just a desire to mark what's mine."

"Does it show?"

"What?"

"Your mark."

"Does it matter?"

"Well, the guys at the club will never let me live it down."

"What club? Do you have a club?"

"Just a figure of speech."

"So is the mark—a figure of speech, I mean."

"No, it's definitely there. I can feel it."

"Good. Then you won't stray."

"Who wants to stray? I know a good thing when I find it, love."

"Which reminds me—" She opened her eyes and rose on her elbow with an effort, frowning down at him.

"Reminds you of what? Have I been caught in another lie?" He opened his eyes and grinned at her.

"I think so." Rebel held on to the frown. "If you didn't want an executive position at Sinclair—before we ran into each other, I mean—then what were you doing in the building in the first place?"

"Oh . . . that." Donovan toyed absently with a strand of her silver-blond hair.

"Yes, that. Well?"

"Look, it's snowing. Isn't that nice?"

"Donovan."

"We can drag the sleigh out of the stables tomorrow, and—"

"Donovan."

He sighed. "You wouldn't want to just let it drop, I suppose?"

"Not really, no."

"You'll think I'm crazy."

"I doubt that. What were you doing at Sinclair?"

Donovan sighed again. "I followed you there."

Rebel knew that her mouth was open. "What?" she asked faintly.

"I saw you in a restaurant having lunch, and I followed you back to the office."

"Donovan, that's crazy."

"Yeah, well. . . . Anyway, I happened to overhear a couple of the staff talking about how you were slated to take over the company. And about an opening for an executive assistant. So I called Marc and made an appointment to talk to him. It was for the next day, and that was when we ran into each other. Not quite by accident, I'll confess."

"You mean you deliberately ran into me?"

"Not exactly. I just put myself into a position where *you* ran into *me*."

"My God," Rebel murmured wonderingly. "You were plotting and planning even then. But, Donovan, you didn't know me!"

Donovan looked thoughtful for a moment, and she could see that he was considering that in his own mind. "No, I did know you," he said finally, musingly. "I can't explain how, but I did know you. It was as if I'd been waiting for something—someone—and when I saw you, a bell went off."

Rebel had silently thanked fate for sending him to her, and now she realized in some amusement that she should have thanked Donovan. Solemnly, she said, "Do you know that I love you?"

"Yes, I do know that," he said conversationally, his

eyes showing something not at all casual. "Finally. It was a long time in coming, but I have to admit that the delay added a certain spice. And I trust you know that the love is returned?"

"There were a few hints of that."

"Just a few?"

"Let's say I'm convinced."

"Well, if you need a few more hints—"

"Donovan, stop that!" She pushed his wandering hand away and pulled on a serious face. "We have one more thing to settle."

"Really?" He didn't sound very interested.

"One at least. This used-to-be rival of ours."

That sobered him. "The company. Honey, if you want to go on running Sinclair—"

"I told you, it's not important to me anymore," she interrupted softly. "I don't have to prove anything now."

He went very still. "Rebel?"

She rested her chin on the hands folded atop his chest and smiled whimsically. "I was thinking that we could look around—maybe in Texas. Find a ranch. Plant a fig tree or two and watch them grow."

"Rebel . . ."

"Merry Christmas, darling . . ."

Chapter 10

REBEL TOTALED THE last column of figures and turned off the calculator. She rubbed the small of her back as she studied the paper in front of her, then flexed her shoulders to ease the slight ache.

"Come to bed, love."

"I'm not sure that's safe." She sent an amused glance across to the man sprawled out on their king-sized bed. "I think you're still mad at me."

"Don't remind me."

Rebel smiled to herself and began putting the ranch records away in her desk. "At least now I know what you're like when you get mad. Very loud." She paused in her tidying up to stare pensively into space. "And you swear a lot, too. Carl said he hadn't heard words like that since he left the navy."

"Carl should be shot for letting you into the corral with Ruffian. He's lucky I didn't fire him. And you're lucky I didn't turn you over my knee."

"Donovan, I only—"

"I know what you 'only'—you've told me. You *only* wanted to see the new stallion. You *only* wanted to see if he hated women the way he hates men. You *only*—"

"All right, all right. But he didn't hurt me. And you scared the poor horse to death charging up like that. He turned tail and ran, and Carl wasn't far behind him. That was the only good thing to come out of the situation: Carl and Ruffian became brothers in terror. They're buddies now."

"You're a funny lady."

"Well, really, Donovan! You stood there swearing for ten solid minutes and never once repeated yourself. When the other shoe dropped, I never expected it to make such a loud thump."

"I was completely justified. In your condition—"

"We've been through this. And stop saying my 'condition,' as if I were in the grip of some dreaded disease. I'm a perfectly healthy woman, darling, and as strong as the proverbial horse. The doctor's more worried about you than me; he said he'd read about it in the medical books but didn't believe it until he met you. I think he's writing a paper on you."

Donovan sighed. "I'm never going to hear the end of this."

Rebel slipped off her robe and crawled into bed beside her husband, allowing a giggle to escape at last. "Well, you kept telling me it was some bug you'd picked up. I had to hear about it from the doctor. And he looked so bemused that I wasn't sure what he was trying to tell me."

"It was something I ate, that's all." Donovan drew her close to him with a long arm and sigh. "The doctor's nuts."

"Is my mother nuts? She noticed the other day when she brought that pizza by and you couldn't stay in the room for more than five minutes. She said that it was touching to see a husband who—um— shared in his wife's pregnancy so thoroughly."

"What do you mean share? You've breezed through the past six months. And stop changing the subject. The point is, you should never have been in that corral. That horse could have killed you. Scared me out of a good ten years."

"Sorry, darling. I won't do it again, I promise."

"The heat out there didn't do you any good, either."

"Donovan."

"Just wanted to make my point."

"You did. And then some."

"Good. While I have stubborn Sinclairs on my mind—"

"Donovan . . ."

"—Bessie said that Marc called today. I thought he and Vanessa had gone back to Paris."

"No, they're still in Dallas. Dad just called to repeat that Josh is doing a fine job running the company— except he's complaining that he can't find a decent secretary. Want a job?"

"I have several, thank you. Running a ranch. Looking after a wife who's as stubborn as she is beautiful. Helping to decorate a nursery. Trying to keep from stepping on those kittens you've adopted. And when Astaire sends us that puppy—"

"You can housebreak him."

"Wonderful. I don't know why Astaire decided that Tosh needed a family at this late stage in his life. And I don't know who named that she-wolf Tiffany—"

"Don't insult Tiffany. Tosh will get you; he's insufferably proud of her."

"I know the feeling. I'm insufferably proud of my she-wolf."

"You know, it's a funny thing," Rebel mused aloud, "but your compliments just don't sound like compliments."

"Shall I rephrase?"

"Unless you want to sleep alone."

"I'm insufferably proud of my beautiful, charming, multitalented wife. How was that?"

"Better."

"I wish she'd take better care of herself and not take chances with dangerous horses. I'm terrified of losing her, you know."

"Well, I could say the same." Rebel snuggled a bit closer to her husband, frowning slightly. "About losing you, I mean. Who decided to help break the three-year-olds to saddle in spite of paying trainers to do it for him?"

"You weren't supposed to hear about that."

"I heard."

"I'm going to fire Carl yet."

"It wasn't Carl; it was Bessie. When she went down there to drag you back here for lunch, she saw what I wasn't supposed to know about. I'm sure that she swore at you all the way back to the house."

"She did. In Spanish."

"I'm not surprised. She says I look terrible in black."

"I was *not* thrown."

"Just trying to fly without a plane, huh?"

"The way you stroke my ego is just wonderful."

Rebel bit back a laugh. It had become a habit, these late-night conversations before the lights went out. Sometimes whimsical, sometimes serious, they were a warm and intimate part of her marriage that she cherished.

"Well," she murmured, "wives are like that."

"Mine is, anyway."

"If you were a Bedouin, you could trade me in on a new model."

"I'd have to throw in a couple of goats and a camel, though."

"Not at all. Arabs are fascinated by blonds. You'd probably even get a tasseled saddle or two."

"Ruffian would love that."

"Only if you wore it instead of making him."

"Never mind. I'll keep you for at least another year."

"Gee, thanks. That's big of you."

"My pleasure." Donovan shifted suddenly and muttered, "What the hell—?" He reached under the covers and withdrew a yellow tabby kitten, who blinked at him sleepily. "Rebel..."

"Well, she was asleep; I didn't have the heart to wake her."

Donovan set the kitten on the floor beside the bed, a gesture she immediately and loudly protested. "She can join her brothers and sisters in the kitchen," he said firmly over the heartbreaking mewing.

"Darling, it's a big house; she'll get lost."

"Rebel..."

"Darling..."

"Dammit."

When Donovan returned from his trip down to the kitchen and climbed back into bed, he said resignedly, "I had to feed them again. Honey, if you adopt one more homeless creature, I swear I'll—"

"Oh, dear..."

"Now what?"

"Rabbits. I went into town this morning, and there was this little boy. His mother told him he had to give them away, and—"

"Where are they?"

"Carl put them in an empty stall for me. They're

white, and the little boy named them Jack and Jill."

"Male and female. And Carl put them in a stall together?"

"Of course he— Oh. I never thought..."

"Great. I'll definitely fire Carl in the morning."

"I suppose we'll be raising rabbits now?"

"I don't think we'll have much choice."

"Sorry, darling."

Donovan sighed. "That's all right. Some wives collect hats; mine collects animals."

"I suppose it's my maternal instincts," Rebel murmured wryly. "They seem to be flourishing."

"Speaking of which..." Donovan rose up on an elbow to gaze down at her. "Have we reached the definite possibility of a firm maybe with the names?"

"Lots of suggestions. Geneva called yesterday."

"Don't tell me. Romeo or Juliet?"

"You're not far wrong. Algernon or Clementine. She said they had definite possibilities."

"Oh, God!"

"That wasn't why she called, though. She called about natural childbirth. I told her we were taking classes."

Donovan groaned. "Don't remind me!"

"Hey, fella, I didn't get into this condition on my own, you know." Rebel pointed to her rounded belly.

"I should hope not," he murmured. "Anyway, I said I'd be brave, didn't I?"

"I'm not sure. Getting that yes from you was like pulling teeth."

"Don't make fun of my cowardice. It isn't wifely."

"Maybe not, but it may be a moot point away. If you keep on 'sharing' my pregnancy, they'll have you up on the table instead of me." She fought to keep from laughing at his expression, adding hastily, "Never mind, darling. We'll get through it together."

"Let's get back to the names," he responded wryly. "It's a safer topic."

"Right," she murmured.

"Dad suggested Daniel or Crystal."

"Mom said Clinton or Nicole."

"We'll pass on Geneva's suggestion."

"Agreed. Astaire voted for Taffy or Tamara."

"What do you expect from a man who names a she-wolf Tiffany?"

Rebel ignored the remark. "Your mother said Jeremy or Selena."

"And your father suggested Logan or Danica."

"Donovan?"

"What?"

"I don't hear a single suggestion from us."

"I've noticed."

"Don't you have a preference?"

"Just a few prejudices. *Not* Algernon or Clementine. And not Puff or Spot. Other than that, I've an open mind."

Rebel sighed. "Well, then, why don't we ask the baby what name to pick."

Donovan looked at her as though he thought the sun might really have gotten to her that day. "Want to run that by me again?"

"You heard me. We can ask the baby." Rebel smiled at him innocently. "Or rather, you can. First, find out the sex. Then ask what name the baby prefers. It'll solve all our problems."

"Rebel . . ."

"Come on, Donovan the Great; pull on your wizard suit and ask the baby for a name."

He lifted an eyebrow to her. "I get this feeling that I'm being taunted. You don't think I can do it."

"Like Alice's queen, I've believed as many as six

impossible things before breakfast," she said gently.

He lifted the other eyebrow. "If you're going to quote, you should remember Shakespeare. You know, the part about there being more things in heaven and earth..."

"I'll keep that in mind."

Donovan shifted position until he could rest one ear against Rebel's rounded stomach. He remained there for a moment, frowning in obvious concentration. A little while later, he was back beside Rebel and drawing her into his arms.

"Well?" She gazed at him laughingly, her arms creeping up around his neck. "Boy or girl?"

"Boy," Donovan informed his wife firmly. "Boys, really. We are going to have twins, love."

"That," Rebel said immediately, "isn't possible. There are no twins in my family, and I've never seen a sign of them in your family. You're wrong this time."

"Twins. Boys."

Looking at her husband's calm face and suspiciously twinkling eyes, Rebel asked mildly, "Did they happen to mention a date? The doctor said October—"

Donovan shook his head. "November third." He paused, tilting his head to one side as though listening to a far-off voice...or voices. Then he added casually, "Between ten and eleven A.M."

Rebel blinked. Vaguely, she remembered a great-uncle who had been able to predict a baby's birth to within a few hours after a single look at a pregnant woman's stomach. Did Donovan possess that curious talent? Or had he—? No, ridiculous.

"Bet you're wrong," she told him. "The doctor, my father, two old ladies I met on the street, *and* Geneva all said that I'd have a girl in October."

Donovan smiled. "Twin boys. Born November third between ten and eleven A.M." When Rebel stared at him, he added, "We'd better start doubling up on supplies. And we'd better be careful with colors. They're redheads."

Rebel felt victory in her grasp. "Now I *know* you're wrong! There is absolutely no way on earth we'll have redheaded *boys*. It won't happen."

"They want to be called Eric and Patrick," Donovan said as if she hadn't spoken.

"No way."

"You don't like the names?"

"They won't have red hair, Donovan. It isn't possible."

"You want me to call my sons liars?"

"They can't have red hair. It'll upset the Indian theory."

"One theory shot to hell."

"We'll have your entire family flying out here to observe the miracle."

"We'll wait until Christmas and then spring it on them."

"You're wrong this time. I *know* you're wrong."

"They're redheads," Donovan repeated stubbornly.

"Care to make a small wager?" Rebel invited spiritedly.

"Certainly. You'll be my slave for a week."

"Or you'll be mine!"

"Agreed, wife."

"Donovan?"

He was busy kissing her neck. "Ummm?"

"Oh . . . never mind. I don't think I want to know."

Patrick Daniel and Eric Shannon Knight were born on November third between ten and eleven A.M. And the doctor, who had been apprised of both the lack of twins in both families and the Indian theory, spent a lot of time muttering to himself.

Tired but happy, Rebel looked at the tiny bundle her husband bent down to place in her arms. She gently stroked the copper-colored fuzz covering the small head and gazed into violet-blue eyes that stared seriously back at her. Then she looked up at Donovan, still wearing his hospital gown, mask dangling, and holding an identical bundle in his own arms.

"What if you'd been wrong?" she asked.

He smiled. "But I wasn't."

"But what if you *had* been?"

"I wasn't."

Under her breath, Rebel said something about six impossible things. Then she murmured, "Donovan, did you really . . . ?"

His violet eyes held tender laughter. "Did I really what, love?"

Rebel thought it over for a moment, then shook her head. "Never mind. I don't think I want to know."

"I had a feeling you'd say that, love . . ."

WATCH FOR 6 NEW TITLES EVERY MONTH!

Second Chance at Love

All of the above titles are $1.75 per copy

SK-41a

WHAT READERS SAY ABOUT
SECOND CHANCE AT LOVE BOOKS

"I can't begin to thank you for the many, many hours of pure bliss I have received from the wonderful SECOND CHANCE [AT LOVE] books. Everyone I talk to lately has admitted their preference for SECOND CHANCE [AT LOVE] over all the other lines."
—*S. S., Phoenix, AZ**

"Hurrah for Berkley . . . the butterfly and its wonderful SECOND CHANCE AT LOVE."
—*G. B., Mount Prospect, IL**

"Thank you, thank you, thank you—I just had to write to let you know how much I love SECOND CHANCE AT LOVE . . . "
—*R. T., Abbeville, LA**

"It's so hard to wait 'til it's time for the next shipment . . . I hope your firm soon considers adding to the line."
—*P. D., Easton, PA**

"SECOND CHANCE AT LOVE is fantastic. I have been reading romances for as long as I can remember—and I enjoy SECOND CHANCE [AT LOVE] the best."
—*G. M., Quincy, IL**

*Names and addresses available upon request